Lucy's
(very COOL, and totally true)
E-Journal

Lucy's
(very COOL, and totally true)
E-Journal

by Jane Harrington

AN
APPLE
PAPERBACK

SCHOLASTIC INC.

New York   Toronto   London   Auckland   Sydney
Mexico City   New Delhi   Hong Kong   Buenos Aires

ISBN 0-439-32373-8

12 11 10 9 8 7 6 5 4 3 2 1   1 2 3 4 5 6/0

Printed in the U.S.A.   40

First Scholastic printing, September 2001

Book design by Steve Scott

To my mother-in-law, the real Grandma Gert

NET-YAK TERMS & EMOTICONS
(Check them out!)

<S>: SMILING
2: TO
4: FOR
411: INFORMATION
8: ATE
AYK: AS YOU KNOW
B-4: BEFORE
B: BE
BBL: BE BACK LATER
BBS: BE BACK SOON
BFF: BEST FRIEND FOREVER
BRB: BE RIGHT BACK
C: SEE
CUL8R: SEE YOU LATER
G2G: GOT TO GO
GR8: GREAT
IC: I SEE
IM: INSTANT MESSAGE
L8: LATE
L8R: LATER
N: AND
N-E: ANY
NW: NO WAY
R: ARE
SYL: SEE YOU LATER
TTFN: TA-TA FOR NOW
TTYL: TALK TO YOU LATER

U: YOU
UR: YOU ARE
WFM: WORKS FOR ME
YKW: YOU KNOW WHAT
YUR: YOUR
ZUP: WHAT'S UP

:-)   HAPPY

:-p   STICKING OUT TONGUE

:-O   HELP ME!

:-(*) ABOUT TO BARF

:-{   KINDA BUMMED

l-o   OUCH!

~:-O   GIMME A BREAK!

]|:-) I RULE!

l-)   HEE-HEE

%(CONFUSED AND SAD

:'-(CRYING

:'-D   SO HAPPY I'M CRYING!

Lucy's
(very COOL, and totally true)
E-Journal

June 22, Thursday:
The First Day of Summer Break

Today I decided to start an E-Journal. And it's not because Dad got this SUPER TERRIFIC computer when his school bought all new computers this spring. And it's not because I actually get to have this computer IN MY ROOM! (Can you believe it?) And it's not because Dad bought me this VERY cool E-Journal software for my VERY good report card, and it has all this neat stuff, like web links, E-mail, and Instant Messaging. No, that's not why I'm starting this E-Journal today.

You want to know WHY? Because I want to!

The fact is, this is sure to be a FREAKY summer — probably the FREAKIEST summer of my life. (And I've been around for over ten years!) So I figure I'll need an

1

outlet, and I think writing about everything that happens will be a good way to deal with it. I've kept diaries and journals FOREVER, but I've NEVER kept one on the computer. This will be awesome.

The last journal I had was in one of those blank books with black pages — the kind you write on with Milky Pens. Anyway, I used to take that one to school, and I would use it during lunch whenever our teacher was mad and made us have "quiet lunch." (Who EVER invented THAT? Lunch is for talking!!) I'd pass the journal around the table to my friends and we'd write our conversations in there. It was almost better than talking, because we could read it over and over. (But don't tell my teacher that.)

Anyway, this E-Journal will be even cooler than that, at least once I figure everything out. I already know how to use the different fonts — ISN'T THIS KIND OF NEAT? This is supposed to be like comics. HERE'S A GOOD ONE. Now, THIS is my favorite — What do you think? I can even make cool wallpaper for the backgrounds. There's also a spell-checker. If only I could bring this computer to school for spelling tests!

Hey! I've got mail!! It just arrived in my E-mail box! I set it up so music will play whenever I get mail. I can program the computer to play any music I want from my CDs. But for now, I'm listening to the music that's in the software package, which is like all 1970s television music. The "Woody Woodpecker" theme is playing right now. I like 1970s stuff, but not as much as I like 1960s stuff. My favorite band is the Beatles. (Of course, I like Britney Spears and N'Sync and the Backstreet Boys, too!) I think I'll record some Beatles music onto the E-Journal next. I better stop writing and see who sent me mail!

? ? ? ? ? ? ? ? ? ? ? ? ? ? ? ? ?

Subj: **Summer ——— finally!!!!!**
Date: 06/22/01 09:16:09am Eastern Daylight Time
From: HipHippie
To: LucyLaLa

Lucy!
Can u beeleeeeeve it???? Summer break is HERE!!!! Isn't this the COOLEST?????
What R U doing? I'm at my dad's house, but only 4 another day N then I go 2 my mom's — AYK! Can I come over 2 yur house?

Get back 2 me FAST!!!!!

BFF,
Taylor

3

Subj: re: **Summer —— finally!!!!!**
Date: 06/22/01 09:18:34am Eastern Daylight Time
From: LucyLaLa
To: HipHippie

Taylor!

Come over! Right now! I have something MAJOR 2 tell U!

BFF,
Lucy

Taylor is my best friend. We've been best friends
since kindergarten. That's five whole years! Well, except for two weeks, one day, and four hours that we
weren't friends at all. That was in February. But I
won't get into that.

You may be wondering what I have to tell Taylor.
And since I got kind of distracted from what I was
saying at the beginning of this entry (and I do get
distracted a lot!), you may also be wondering how I
know this is going to be a FREAKY summer. (Of

4

course, you're just a box with wires and a computer chip and stuff, so I guess you can't really WONDER anything. But I'm going to talk to you like you're a real person. Why not? It's MY journal!) There are four main reasons why this summer is going to be FREAKY, and one of those is also what I have to tell Taylor. So, here goes. . . .

REASON NUMBER ONE

Grandma Gert moved in with us last week. She has this disease called Alzheimer's (at first, I thought everyone was saying "Old-Timers"). Her brain doesn't work just right, and she doesn't act at all like a grandmother. Grandmothers are supposed to take you out shopping and let you get the things your mom and dad won't get you, and they're supposed to always, always remember your birthday and to give you brand-new one-dollar bills for your report cards. (That's how my other grandmother is.)

But Grandma Gert has trouble remembering things. She asks the same questions over and over all day long. It wasn't a big deal answering the question "How old are you, dear?" the first ten times she asked it (which was the day she got here), but now I'm totally tired of it. I was ten last week, I'm ten today, and I'll be ten every day until September 16th! And if she asks me ten times a day, from now until my birthday, well, I will have told her my age . . . (10 weeks of summer plus a couple more before my birthday comes to about 12 weeks, times 7 days per week equals 84 days, then multiply that by 10 for how many times a day she asks . . .) 840 times!!!!

My dad talked to us before she moved in. Grandma Gert is his mom. He told us we were lucky we'd be able to spend time with her, because we hardly ever saw her when she lived in Connecticut. It was a real long drive, so it was hard for us to do it much, and Grandma hadn't been traveling for a long time. Dad said she got lost in the airport once when she came for Thanksgiving, but it must have been a while ago, because I don't remember that.

Dad asked us to be real polite and respectful to Grandma, and to say things slowly and loudly (her ears aren't working so well), because he says this is an important family thing that we're doing. And I am trying to be polite and respectful, but it's hard! Sometimes when she asks me a question I've an-swered already, I want to scream!

Journals are for feelings, right? They're for say-ing what's really going on in your mind. They're for exploding when you can't explode anywhere else, right? Well, then, I'll be honest. I DON'T WANT MY GRANDMA LIVING HERE WITH US! I know that isn't nice, but it's the truth. She acts weird and that can be real embarrassing. I wish she'd go live some-where else. Don't tell anyone I said that, please.

REASON NUMBER TWO

There are, like, a billion people living in my house. It's true that you might not count that many if you're doing a bed check at night, but, well, some people come and go. Like the person my dad hired to hang around with Grandma Gert. Her name's Norka and she's real nice and all, but I'm just not used to having her around yet. She's a "companion," which is something that people with Alzheimer's need, so there's someone there to tell them what day it is and where they live and everything, be-cause they forget those kinds of things all the time. Norka is real patient, and she answers Grandma's questions over and over and over. And she speaks Spanish AND English, which is a cool thing, I guess. I like languages, but the only one I know is English. Well, I know Pig Latin, too. At-thay oesn't-day, ount-cay, ough-thay. (I said: "That doesn't count, though.") I don't know why it doesn't count. Why aren't there classes in Pig Latin at school? There should be. At least I think so.

Well, anyway, some of the other billion people around our house recently were the tree-killers, patio-makers, and gardeners who were in the backyard for months, ripping up the grass that I LOVED and taking down the walnut tree that I LOVED, and putting in a patio and garden that I HATE. My mom told me that Grandma would have slipped all the time on those walnuts the tree dropped on the ground, but I really loved the walnuts. That one tree would drop about a thousand of them, easy — I'm sure of it. And some years they were as big as tennis balls! I always liked playing games with them, like throwing them across the yard into different baskets and having prizes for the most points. Once we did it at one of my birthday parties. Total fun. And Emma, my twelve-year-old sister who is a baseball player (yes, with BOYS!), liked the walnuts, too, and used them to practice pitching. Of course, she wasn't allowed to do that after she broke a window. Well, that doesn't matter now that the walnut tree was cut down and a patio was put in its place.

SOOOOO, anyway, in addition to Dad, Mom, me (Lucy), Emma, Grandma, and the others I've just mentioned, there's my teenage sister, Meghan, who CLEARLY should be counted as more than one person. On a good day, she and her friends make as much noise as TEN people, and on a bad day — when she's in one of those moods — she's like FORTY people, easy. More on that later, I'm sure. . . .

REASON NUMBER THREE
(This is the thing I have to tell Taylor!)

Mr. Owen, who lived next door to us, died a couple months ago, so his house is for sale. And guess whose parents I saw looking at the house last week? Billy's!!! If he moves in, I'll have to dig a hole in my backyard, cover it with sticks, and just live there, camouflaged and hidden, forever, so he can't find me and bug me like he always does at school. Summer, I thought, would be my chance to escape from him. I can't think of anything worse than Billy being my next-door neighbor. (!!!!!!)

Taylor lives just two houses down from Mr. Owen's house, so she will FLIP OUT over this, too!!!! She feels the same way about him as I do. At least now she does. She thought she liked him in February. Just like I thought I liked him before that. Actually, right up until Valentine's Day. But I won't get into that right now. Boy, were we stupid!

REASON NUMBER FOUR
My family isn't going to the beach this summer. WE ALWAYS GO TO THE BEACH!! I LOVE the beach!!! You know where I'm going instead? CAMP!!!! And I don't mean, like, daytime archaeology camp, but an OVERNIGHT camp! I've never been to overnight camp! It's, like, ALL NIGHT, EVERY NIGHT, so you

sleep there!!! For THREE solid weeks I'll be stranded in the woods!! With no one I know!!

Well, unless you count Emma, who's going with me. But we don't get along very well, so she isn't going to help much. She's always accusing me of stealing her things (which I don't do — I just borrow stuff now and then), so she goes into my room and randomly takes stuff, just to get back at me.

We're going to camp at the very end of July, which means I'll spend, like, almost all summer worrying about it, then I'll be away for the last weeks of my summer vacation, then I'll have to go RIGHT back to school!

Can you believe it?

Okeday, I'm done with the reasons.

Have you noticed that I say "okeday" instead of "okay"? If you don't know what that's from, you really need to be seeing more movies.

Now for my E-Journal rules and goals . . .

RULÈS

First of all, I'm NOT writing every day. I can't stand something I have to do every day, like washing my face and brushing my teeth and brushing my hair. I'll write once a week, maybe twice, but that's it!

Another rule will be . . . well, I can't think of any

others right now. I'll get back to you on that. I've never really liked rules, actually. So why am I having rules????

I've changed my mind, and the only rule is . . . NO RULES!!!!!

GOALS

My teacher this year, Ms. P., was REAL into goals. She made all of us decide what we're going to be when we grow up. I told Ms. P. I'm going to be a ferret breeder. My whole life I've wanted just one thing: a ferret. A cute, wiggly, furry ferret. But, NOOOOOOOOO — my mom and dad won't let me have one. I've asked for one EVERY birthday of my whole entire life as long as I've been alive — or at least as long as I could talk — and what do I get? Stupid unalive things.

(Well, the lava lamp isn't stupid. And the Beatles' *Yellow Submarine* poster isn't stupid. But you know what I mean . . .)

This summer my goal is to make my mom and dad see that I NEED a ferret. Ms. P. says that when you pick a goal, you have to stick to it, that you can do ANYTHING if you really try.

I sure hope Ms. P. knows what she's talking about.

(Maybe she'll get me a ferret if my mom and dad don't come through.)

Someone's pounding on the door downstairs. I hope it's Taylor. She won't believe that Billy might be moving to Oak Street! She'll die when I tell her!!!

:- (*)

June 26, Monday

Today the STRANGEST thing happened. I woke up feeling homesick — like when I stay at Aunt Katey's apartment in New York City. But here's the ridiculous part: I WAS HOME. So I figured out that since I was missing something, it must be school. I obviously was school-sick. And I still am. I've got that longing feeling inside me that sort of makes me feel like I'm inside out. I miss Lauren and Justin and Tajuana. I miss all my school friends. I see some friends around here, but not that many. My school is in Old Town, and almost all of the kids take buses to get there (like I do), so I don't even know where some of my friends live.

Now that I really think about this, though, there are things I don't miss about school. Like I don't

miss being freezing cold in my air-conditioned class-
room when it's the perfect kind of hot outside. And I
definitely don't miss that new crisis teacher in the
school who seems to BE the crisis, if you ask me.
She's supposed to counsel us and take care of big
problems, but the way she's always bossing
everyone around, she just gets kids upset and that
makes MORE problems. She doesn't seem to understand kids at all. Emma REALLY can't stand her.
Emma says she's glad to be going to middle school
in the fall. Even though we don't always get along, I'll
miss Emma when she goes to her new school. Then
I'll be Emma-sick.

Anyway, there's other stuff I don't miss about
school. How about getting up so early in the morning? I definitely don't miss that. Peanut butter and
jelly sandwiches? Sick of that. And I don't miss Char-
lie or Andrew, and (OF COURSE) I don't miss Billy at
all. It's because of Billy that Taylor and I stopped being friends for two weeks, one day, and four hours
last February. But I won't go into that.

Speaking of Billy, GUESS what happened last
night? Billy actually was in my yard. He was next
door looking at Mr. Owen's house with his parents
(which is really a bad sign, I think), and he actually
came over. I can't believe he would have the nerve!!!!
And Dad told me this morning that Billy's parents are

making an offer on the house. I'm not sure what that means, but it doesn't sound good. I'm going to look for a shovel today and start digging that big hole to hide in.

Let me tell you the story of what happened last night. Some of it is funny and some is not! It's a true life-story, and I'm calling it . . .

BuGs iN My BAckYaRd

Last night I was catching fireflies, which I was planning to feed to Emma's pet toad (which is the COOLEST thing — did you know that when toads eat fireflies you can actually see the bugs light up INSIDE their bellies? I'm not making this up). ANYWAY — I had about six bugs in a jar and I was just about to catch another one in the sunflower patch next to the new patio in the backyard when Billy jumped out in front of me and yelled, "Hi, Lucy-Goosey!"

I HATE THAT! I DOUBLE-HATE THAT AND TRIPLE-HATE THAT!

And so, of course, I dropped the jar and it crashed on the patio, which is made of slate, so it is VERY hard. (Not like it USED to be when it was grass. I could drop anything on the grass and it wouldn't break!) So glass was everywhere, and the fireflies blinked away all around me.

I wanted to get out of there fast, because Billy

was still standing there, and he was laughing at me now, but you know what? I couldn't move! I was frozen in place because of my bare feet. (I like to be barefoot in the summer. I hid my shoes the day school let out.) There was NOWHERE I could step without cutting my feet. So I stood there, getting madder and madder at Billy, and at the patio being there at all.

"Get out of here, Billy!!!" I yelled.

"It's Bill," he said.

(He recently decided that he wants to be called "Bill" instead of "Billy." I don't know what's up with that. But I also don't care.)

"Get OUT of here, Billy!" I said again.

"I'm moving in next do-or," he said in that really annoying singsong way.

Well, even though I was supermad, and I couldn't move, I was thinking. I said in a real mysterious way, "I don't think you know everything about that house."

"Like what?" he asked.

"That real estate person didn't tell you what happened?" I said.

I was hoping he would give me some long answer, because I needed time to figure out where I was going with this. But he didn't give me any answer. He just looked at my feet and laughed some more.

"Maybe you should look in the attic next time you go in the house," I said.

"Why?" he asked, not laughing now. "What's in the attic?"

"All I'm going to say is, everyone thinks he didn't have any children, but, well, he had ONE," I said, holding my index finger up in front of his face and sounding VERY serious. Billy was looking nervous. I decided to keep talking. (The story was doing a very good job of making itself up.)

"He had one son about forty years ago, and people say the kid was always around, playing on the block," I continued. "The neighbors say they saw him until he was, oh, about ten, and then all of a sudden they stopped seeing him. And when they asked Mr. Owen about it, he said he didn't know what they were talking about, that he didn't HAVE any children."

Billy's eyes opened wider. "Didn't the neighbors call the police?" he asked.

"Mr. Owen was captain of the police force," I answered.

(Quick thinking, huh?)

I went on.

"After his son disappeared, Mr. Owen started being real mean to all the kids on the block, especially boys, and especially ten-year-old boys. AND he

17

wouldn't let anyone go up in the attic," I said in kind of a whispery voice.

Billy was looking definitely scared. I was real happy. And then I noticed, behind him, Grandma Gert's cat creeping up. This is a big cat, too, and totally white. Like a ghost. I got ANOTHER idea.

"The neighbors also told me that Mr. Owen was convinced he was going to come back to life as a CAT," I said in that same kind of whispery voice, and at the VERY moment I said "cat" that big old cat rubbed against Billy's bare leg. Boy, did he JUMP! AND SCREAM!! It was GREAT!!!! (Billy's the biggest wimp I've ever met, by the way.)

It was MY turn to laugh, and he got all huffy and said my story was stupid and he didn't believe me.

"And ferrets are stupid, too," he said, storming across the patio, broken glass crunching under his sneakers.

"Grrrr . . ." I growled, looking at that most hated person as he disappeared around the corner of the house.

Once he was gone, I broke a big sunflower off at the base and used it as a broom to clear a path through the broken glass, and I went into the house to find a new jar. I could see through the front window that Billy was getting into his parents' car. He was talking to them and pointing at Mr. Owen's house. He definitely looked worried.

ANd ThAt's tHe EnD oF tHaT sToRy.

I hear someone out in the hall. It's Emma, I think, and I don't want her reading my E-Journal. It's private!

A good thing about this computer is that it's in my room, but a bad thing about it is that Emma and I are supposed to share it. The reason I got to have it in MY room is that I don't have as much stuff on my desk. Emma has her toad tank and a new tank with a baby box turtle. (Mom works at a nature center, and people are always giving her animals they don't know what to do with. Sometimes she brings them home. We have a huge corn snake in our dining room, and a leopard gecko in the living room.) Mom offered the baby box turtle to me, but I'm afraid to accept one of those pets because then the next time I ask for a ferret, she can say, "But you have a pet already," or something totally parentish like that. A kid needs to be careful. . . .

So, anyway, Emma's pretty jealous that I got the computer in my room. Dad gave her some software for it (a sports game thing that I'm not allowed to use), and she's not supposed to use my E-Journal software or look at my files. I'm sure she's trying to read them anyway — she'd do that to get me back for when I used to borrow things. So, to be extra careful, I'm saving my E-Journal entries only on disk, and I'm hiding the disk under my mattress. I wonder if there's a website about catching sisters snooping in your private stuff. Maybe other kids in the world are having this same problem and can give me some ideas about catching her in the act. Maybe I could make my own website. I'd call it WWW.NOLOOKING.SIS.

Emma's in her room now, which is right next to mine. I know she's in there because she's throwing a ball against the wall. Emma spends most of her time down at the park with her friends — who are mostly BOYS. They play basketball, baseball, kickball, and lots of other stuff. I think the only reason Emma's home today is because it's raining.

Meghan's home, too, which isn't so unusual. She always hangs out in her room, which is in the attic, which is right above my room. She usually has friends up there — but no boys. Mom and Dad won't let her have boys in her room, even though she asks. Today she has about five friends up there, and they're watching a movie, listening to CDs, and talking in really loud voices to one another AND on the phone.

It is WAY loud right now with the BANG (pause) BANG (pause) BANG of Emma's ball, and all those

teenage voices and the music, and I can't even s
my door. You want to know why? Because my parents said one of the rules about having the computer in my room is that we aren't allowed to shut
the door when we're on the Internet. What do they
think is going to happen? Do they think an Internet
monster is going to burst out of the computer and
grab me and pull me in? How random is that? (Well,
that would make a GREAT story, wouldn't it?)

I'm going web-surfing.

BRB

🚲 🚲 🚲 🚲 🚲 🚲 🚲 🚲 🚲 🚲 🚲 🚲 🚲 🚲 🚲 🚲 🚲

I'm back from cyberspace now. I LOVE THE
INTERNET!! It's AWESOME!!!! I found a website
about — you guessed it — FERRETS! It's at
WWW.FURRYFERRETS.ORG. You can learn all about
ferrets on it, join a ferret club, and even download a
virtual ferret into your computer.

There's also a ferret photo gallery on the website. I looked at ALL the pictures. Some are from a
picnic that was just for people and their ferrets.
(LUCKY PEOPLE!!!)

I want a ferret!!!

:-)

June 28, Wednesday

Now I'm going to tell you about Grandma's cat.

(Norka says the Spanish word for cat is *gato*. Now I know three ways to say cat: CAT, GATO, and AT-CAY.)

Grandma brought her cat here with her when she moved in. I remember when he was a kitten, a long time ago. I used to play with him whenever we visited Grandma in Connecticut. He had a catnip ball and we thought it was real funny the way he rolled around and acted crazy when he played with it. So when Dad told us that Grandma was moving in, I first thought of the cat. I love animals — especially furry ones — so I was SUPERglad to have a cat move in. And I remembered that I loved the name Grandma had given him. He was called Milky Way.

I say "was" because Grandma doesn't call him Milky Way anymore. She calls him Pharaoh, which Dad told me is the name of a cat she had thirty years ago. It was a Siamese cat and looked NOTH-ING like Milky Way, but somehow the cats got all jumbled up in her mind, and, well, she thinks Milky Way is Pharaoh. I really don't like that. It must be confusing for the cat.

The name switcheroo wasn't the first different thing I noticed about the cat, though. The first thing was that the cat was about ten times fatter than he was the last time I'd seen him. I think the cat has a memory problem, too, because he seems to always forget that he's just eaten. And Grandma forgets that she's just fed him. And, believe it or not, it goes on like that the whole day, every day. The cat's HUGE.

And that's not all. The other cats in the neighbor-hood are getting pretty large, too. Grandma feeds Milky Way inside AND outside, and so cats from blocks around have heard about it from some kind of cat network (maybe they have a kitty website — WWW.CAT.EAT), and cats are always in the back-yard. Dad calls it the all-day cat buffet (pronounced "buff-ay," so it rhymes). And it's not just cat food. Grandma puts pancakes, yogurt, apple slices, and just about anything out for the cats. Milky Way will eat all of it. I'm not joking.

The food out there doesn't only attract cats, either. For some reason, yellow jackets like the food, and birds (starlings, mostly) and flies are real into it. Especially when it's the canned kind. At night the cockroaches come, too, and raccoons and possums. Mom says one of us should take up wildlife photography. She told me that you can get pictures sent to your E-mail address so you can have an on-screen photo album. I wish I had a picture of my sister Meghan yesterday. That would be real funny. But since I don't, I'm going to tell you a story about that. I'll call it . . .

ThE CaT DiShEs

When Meghan got up yesterday morning (actually, it was afternoon, which is when she gets up during summer), she had a really LOUD and TOTAL fit. I think what happened is that she couldn't find a cereal bowl anywhere in the kitchen, so she opened the back door (maybe to find Dad or something). I was outside at the time, riding my bike in the driveway, which is what I do when I'm bored. When I heard the screaming I pedaled my bike over to check it out and saw Meghan standing in the doorway. From the sound of her, I thought there were aliens in the house, or that her phone was broken, but it wasn't that. She was SCREAMING because every single one of our cereal bowls was outside, filled with cat food or pudding or hot dogs, and covered in flies and bees and other crawly things. On top of that, fat cats were prowling around all over the backyard.

It was ugly.

Grandma Gert appeared and cheerfully said she would wash a bowl for Meghan, and she picked up an especially horrible one with dried-up cat food stuck to the sides. A cockroach crawled out of it, and Meghan grabbed at her heart and screamed again and leaned against the door like she was going to faint.

I got off my bike and went in. I wasn't bored anymore.

Grandma took the bowl to the sink, put some water in it, and rubbed it a little with the sponge and then dried it with a towel. There was still gunk stuck to the sides of the bowl, but she smiled and offered it to Meghan, who stared for a second, then ran up the stairs screaming, "DA-A-A-D!!!"

I think what REALLY got to Meghan was the fact that Grandma hadn't used any soap when she was cleaning the bowl. That seems to be one of the things Grandma has forgotten about life. She LOVES to do the dishes and wants to do ALL our dishes — even though we have a dishwasher — but she never uses the dish soap that's right there next to the sink. Dad always suggests it when he's around, but she looks at him like he's just asked her to wash the dishes with slime or something.

ANYWAY . . . I went upstairs a few steps behind Meghan to see what was going to happen next. She was totally FREAKED, telling Dad about the whole thing, and how she was NEVER going to be able to eat in the house again. I just watched, thinking how lucky I am that Dad's a teacher and he's home in the summer. She might have been yelling at me if he hadn't been there.

Dad just nodded and said, "We need real cat dishes. Then Grandma won't need to use the cereal bowls. Want to go with me to Pet Village?"

"YES!!" I screamed. I knew he wasn't talking to me, but, hey, I never miss a chance to go to Pet Village. Guess what they have there?????!!!

(If you guessed ferrets, you're RIGHT!!!)

Meghan told Dad she'd leave that up to him, that she was too tired from lack of proper nutrition — or something like that — and she'd watch TV until we got back.

At Pet Village Dad went to the cat dish aisle, and I went straight to the ferret cages. They had two ferrets, which were babies, and they wanted to go home with me SOOOOO much, I could tell. One looked right at me and then did a flip. I'm pretty certain that means "I want to be your pet" in ferret language. I decided to go tell Dad about that.

I went to the cat dish aisle and Dad was standing there looking at the shelves. There were tons of dishes. Dad was rubbing his mustache, which he does when he's thinking.

"Dad, come on," I said. "I've got to show you something."

But he kept looking at the dishes. "It's got to look like a cat dish and not a cereal bowl," he said.

"How about this one?" I said, taking a metal one off the shelf.

"Not obvious enough," he answered.

I just wanted him to make up his mind so he could go see the ferrets, so I looked harder for the right kind of dish. One that a person would KNOW was a cat dish. Then I saw it! I grabbed it and showed it to Dad. It was white, with a big purple picture of a cat right in the bottom, and on the outside it said, in very big letters, CAT DISH.

"Good choice," he said, and he grabbed another five of them off the shelf and asked me to grab as many as I could carry, and started walking toward the checkout lines.

"Da-a-ad," I pleaded. "You've got to come SEE something!"

"See what?" he asked.

As if he didn't KNOW.

"Come HERE," I said, pushing him from behind, straight to the ferret cage.

I pointed to the flippy little guy. "He told me he wants to be my pet."

"What do you want a weasel for?" he asked.

"Dad!! You know they're not weasels!!" He always says something totally stupid whenever I ask for a ferret.

My dad looked at me. I saw sympathy in his eyes. He opened his mouth. I KNEW he was going to give in this time! I KNEW that he was ready to make me a happy person. He was finally going to say YES!!!

He said, "Lucy, I know you want a ferret, but they need a lot of attention, and we've already got so much going on in our house."

Like that's my fault!

Then Dad announced that we should get a case of cat food while we were there, and he went to find that. I started after him, then noticed a book on a rack by the ferret cage. It had a most adorable picture of baby ferrets on the front cover.

"Will you at least get me a book, so I can see what kind of *attention* ferrets need?" I called after Dad.

He didn't refuse. He loves books, and I'm supposed to read books over the summer, so why not one about ferrets?

I looked at the precious pictures of ferrets all the way home.

(Guess what? This E-Journal also has a built-in thesaurus for finding words with the same meanings. I just got that word "precious" from it. I didn't want to use the word "adorable" again, and so now I have a NEW word for describing ferrets!)

In the kitchen, Dad stacked the cat dishes in the middle of the counter and made a tall pyramid of cat food cans right next to them.

"That should do it," he said.

I agreed. It was the most obvious thing in the entire world. Cat food dishes and cat food. Together.

"The cereal bowls will be safe," he announced, picking up all the disgusting bowls from outside the back door.

He scrubbed each one with dish soap and hot water and put all of them in the drying rack. Then he went upstairs to show Meghan one of the new cat bowls, and to tell her that it was safe to eat again.

I went outside to sit on the garden swing. (All right, I like THAT part of the new garden, but I'd STILL rather have my walnut tree!) I sat, swinging back and forth, and I read the first chapter of the ferret book, "Is a Ferret Right for You?" It said that ferrets live eight to ten years and that they can live with other animals, like cats.

I looked around the garden. There were about five cats hanging around, and Milky Way was standing right at the back door. Waiting for food, I figured. I decided to go find Grandma and tell her about the new dishes and the cat food.

I did find Grandma. She was in the dining room, eating a bowl of cereal. And do you know what bowl she was eating out of? I'm NOT making this up, either! She had one of those CAT bowls, with the BIG letters that say CAT DISH, and she was just finishing her cereal, so the purple cat at the bottom of the bowl was looking right up at her.

Just then I heard Meghan coming down the stairs (which sounds like an elephant stampede), and she appeared in the dining room, looked at Grandma there scooping cereal out of one of those cat dishes, and then she got some kind of weird look on her face. I can't really describe it too well. It was horror and something else, too. I'll try my thesaurus, by looking up "horror."

Okeday, my thesaurus gave me the word "revulsion." Meghan had a look of revulsion on her face. That sounds right.

ANYWAY, Dad came in behind Meghan, and he

looked at everyone a second, and then just burst out laughing. Then I started laughing. Then Grandma started laughing, but I'm not sure she knew why. She just likes to laugh, and I like her laugh. It's sort of like this hooting sound. I was thinking we were like those people in *Mary Poppins* who laugh so hard they go up to the ceiling.

But Meghan wasn't laughing. The look on her face turned to a totally annoyed look, and she stomped upstairs saying something about how she was going to starve to death.

We stopped laughing.

Grandma looked at me and smiled. "How old are you, dear?" she asked.

Dad put his hand on my shoulder.

"Ten," I answered, smiling, with my teeth clenched. I had answered that question FIVE times already, and the day was young.

"What's in there?" Grandma asked, pointing to the corn snake's tank in the corner of the room.

She'd asked THAT question four times. I was keeping count.

"Hey!" Dad cried. "Guess what we bought today, Mom!"

He helped Grandma out of the chair and led her into the kitchen and showed her the pyramid of cat food and the rest of the cat dishes on the counter.

He filled one of the dishes with cat food — in front of Grandma — so she might remember the next time — and we put it outside for the cats.

AnD ThAt's tHe EnD oF tHat sToRy.

It's sure weird living with Grandma, but it CAN be entertaining sometimes.

:-p

July 1, Saturday

Oh, no!!!! I can't believe it!!! It's already JULY!!!
Where is summer vacation going? Before I know it,
it'll be time to go to camp! Last night at dinner Mom
asked me if I was looking forward to it. She tried to
tell me all these "great" things about the camp, that
it's got a zip wire (whatever THAT is), and there'll be
hiking and boating and rock climbing and stuff. I'll
probably break my legs. Then she'll be sorry!

Taylor is coming over today. I haven't seen her
all week, because she's been at her mom's house.
It's kind of tough having a best friend who's gone
every other week. It's been like that since second
grade, when her parents got divorced. Her mom
didn't move that far away, but it's far enough that I
never seem to see her when she's over there — I

can't walk there, so it just doesn't happen. Her dad talks about moving sometimes, too. Like every time he has to clean the house, he says he's moving to a smaller house. He even goes to look at houses sometimes, but Taylor always talks him out of it. Good thing! I'D DIE IF MY BEST FRIEND MOVED AWAY FROM OAK STREET! I know her house is much bigger than they need, since it's just the two of them, and Taylor isn't even there half the time. But I need to have Taylor close by. Once I asked her dad if I could move in. He thought I was kidding.

Even when Taylor is at her mom's, we talk every day on the phone or on the Internet. That's because we're super-super-best friends. We haven't missed one single day talking to each other in all the years we've been best friends. Well, except maybe when we're on vacation, but we send postcards. And then, of course, there was that two weeks, one day, and four hours that we didn't talk at all. That's history, though. And I don't want to talk about it. That could NEVER happen again.

Anyway, today Taylor is going to help me catch Emma stealing my stuff. You see . . . I have this box I keep my candy in. It's a cool box, with flower-power flowers all over it. (I got it for my birthday last year.) I filled up the box on the last day of school with candy I got from Ms. P., and I don't eat candy very fast, so I figured it would last a long time. (Usually my Halloween candy lasts until the winter holidays when I get more.) EMMA, though, eats candy VERY fast. HER Halloween candy is usually gone by Thanksgiving, and she gets twice as much as I do, because Mom and Dad let her go to more places than I'm allowed to go to. And she and her friends RUN from door to door, so they can get the most candy. They should dress up for Halloween as PIGS!

Back to my box of candy —

It had eighteen Hershey Kisses in it, and six Hugs. I know this. I counted them on the last day of school. Then I ate one Kiss each day, that's all. I didn't eat ANY of the Hugs. (I like them best, and I was saving them.) So, yesterday, I counted the candies again. There were only SIX Kisses, and FOUR Hugs. There SHOULD have been NINE Kisses and SIX Hugs, because yesterday was only the ninth day since school let out. Sooo, someone has been eating my candy. And I'm sure it's Emma. I mean, who else could it be?

Also, I want to find out if Emma has found my E-Journal disk. So, today I'm putting a piece of clear tape over the crack between my mattress and the bed, where Emma won't notice it. If she lifts up my mattress she'll rip the tape (not knowing it), and if I find the tape apart, I'll know she's been snooping around for my disk. (I got this idea because Dad put tape on the door of the house once to make sure Meghan wasn't sneaking out with her friends at night. I thought it was a cool detective idea.)

By the end of the day, I'll have plenty of proof that Emma is not only a SNOOP, but also a THIEF. I'll present my evidence at dinner. Surely Mom and Dad won't THINK of sending me off to camp with Emma once they know the truth!

Taylor is here now. She brought her binoculars over, which is a great idea. She thinks we can find a place outside to sit and hide and watch the box of candy through the binoculars. We put the box right at the window, and now we are going to go find my mom so I can borrow her binocs. But I won't tell anyone what we are doing, because I don't want to risk Emma finding out!!!

I think, on the way out, we'll also suggest to Emma that she has lots of time to play on the computer today, since Taylor and I are going out to observe wildlife (ha-ha).

Taylor is ready with the clear tape, and I'm getting ready to save my file and put the disk under my mattress. We're going to spread the blanket over the bed real neatly, so Emma doesn't see the tape.

The next time I write in this, I will have the proof I need! I KNOW it!

¡Adios! (Norka taught me that. It's Spanish for "good-bye.")

🐱🐱🐱🐱🐱🐱🐱🐱🐱🐱🐱🐱🐱🐱🐱🐱🐱

I'm writing before bed. Boy, did it turn out to be a STUPID day! And even though this is going to be a TOTALLY stupid story, I am going to tell it anyway. I'll call it . . .

ThE VeRy sTuPiDeSt DaY ThAt cOuLd EvER bE

Taylor and I went outside with our binoculars right after lunch, and we tried lots of spots in the yard, to see if we could spy on my box of candy, but everywhere we stood was too low, because my bedroom is upstairs. And, of course, there is no tree in our yard to climb anymore! (Mom planted a maple tree next to the patio, but it will be a long time before it'll be big enough to climb — I'll probably be GROWN UP. Who climbs trees when they're grown up?) We went over to Mr. Owen's yard, where there's a crabapple tree. It's easy to climb, and so we were up in the branches in no time, and settled on a good limb, and we could see my window through the binocs, and everything was perfect. We took turns watching, and since nothing was happening at first, we just talked about things that had gone on during the week Taylor was at her mother's house. We talked about how I scared Billy with the story of Mr. Owen's son and the cat-ghost, and I told her I hadn't seen him since that night and that I was hoping his parents had decided not to buy the house.

Then, out of nowhere, Billy showed up in the yard.

We decided to stay real quiet, because the leaves of the tree hid us really well, and we thought Billy wouldn't notice us. He was looking around, and he had something in his hand, and it jingled. We looked through the binocs, and we could see that it was a cat collar with a bell! He was going to put a BELL on Milky Way!

"See," I whispered to Taylor, "he's scared of the cat."

"What a wimp!" Taylor whispered back.

"Kitty, kitty, kitty," we could hear Billy saying in that squeaky kind of voice you use with pets.

He sounded stupid, and we started to giggle, but then stopped ourselves right away. He looked

up, but maybe he just thought it was a bird or something, because he started right back in "kitty-kitty-
ing" around the yard.

"You have to have food to get that cat's attention," I whispered to Taylor.

"You watch Billy, and I'll keep an eye on your window," Taylor whispered back to me. She was right.
We might miss something if we didn't keep an eye
on the window every second, and we HAD to watch
Billy, too. We didn't want him sneaking up on us.

Milky Way was, of course, sitting by my back
door, waiting for a fresh bowl of food, probably his
fifth of the day. It didn't take Billy long to spot him
there, and so he tiptoed toward him, meowing and
making other cat sounds. When he got right up next
to Milky Way, he bent over and scratched the cat's
back, which Milky Way seemed to like, because he
dropped on the ground and rolled around.

Well, Billy was there, all bent over, with his back
end pointed right at us, and BOY did I wish I had my
Super Soaker with me. Then I noticed that there
were lots of green crab apples on the tree. They
were small, but real HARD. I could only see his back-
side, but it looked like he was about done fastening
the collar, so I had to act fast. I picked one, aimed,
and PING! I couldn't believe it. It hit him right on target!

He jumped up and turned around, and I looked through the binocs at his face, which looked REAL mad.

"Uh-oh," Taylor whispered.

"He deserved it," I whispered back, giggling.

"Deserved what?" Taylor asked.

She hadn't seen my amazing shot. She had been looking at my candy box the whole time. Which is what she was supposed to be doing. Which is what she had said "uh-oh" about.

"Look at your window," she said to me.

I pointed my binocs at my window just in time to see MY DAD putting the top back on my candy box. And he stood there, unwrapped the KISS or the HUG (I couldn't tell at the time), and ate it!!!! My own father!!!!! A thief!!!!

"I can't believe it!" I said, and I guess I forgot to whisper, because Billy looked right at the tree then and started yelling.

"Is that you, Lucy-Goosey?"

"Get out of my yard!" I yelled.

"Get out of my tree!" he yelled back.

"It's not YOUR tree," I yelled back.

"Yes it is. My parents put a contract on the house yesterday, and that means I'm going to live here!" He was laughing now.

"Oh no!" Taylor said.

40

"Who else is up there, Mr. Owen's son?" he asked. He was under the tree now, looking right up at us.

"Yeah, he's my new boyfriend, and he's going to turn you into a zombie," I said. "His bones are in the attic — have you looked yet?"

"Oh, sure, like I'd really find anything," he said. "Is that Taylor up there? I'm going to be YOUR neighbor, too, Taylor!"

At least she would have a house in between her house and his, I thought.

I yelled something back at him, but I was starting to feel a little nervous. We were kind of stuck up in that tree, with nowhere to go, and Billy at the bottom.

"Uh-oh," Taylor said again.

"I know," I whispered. "WHAT are we going to DO?"

"No, 'uh-oh' is about your candy again," she said.

I looked back at the window and couldn't believe it. Now my MOM was taking candy out of my box!!!!!

I had to get out of the tree, and right away. My parents were in BIG TROUBLE.

"Pelt him!" I yelled, and I began grabbing big handfuls of crab apples from the branches. Taylor did the same, and we chucked them down as hard as we could. At first he grabbed them back from the ground and threw them up at us, but his aim was terrible, and then Taylor threw one that hit him right in the nose, hard, and that made him cry. He ran off down the street screaming that he was going to tell her father.

I felt pretty bad. I know I shouldn't hurt anyone. Taylor said she wasn't aiming for his face. We both were sorry, but sometimes it's just too hard to be good. And anyway, what kind of example do my parents set? Candy thieves, both of them!

We scrambled down the tree and went in the back door of the house, Milky Way right at our heels. (I knew this because of the stupid bell that was dinging when he walked.) Grandma was doing the dishes.

"Hello, Pharaoh! And hello, dear," she said, first to the cat, then to me. "How old are you now?"

"Grandma, his name is MILKY WAY and I'm TEN!" I yelled, zipping down the hall and up the stairs. I know I wasn't exactly polite and respectful, but I was in a hurry.

Emma was in my room on the computer, and I went right up to her and smelled her breath to see if SHE had been stealing my candy, too. I couldn't smell any chocolate, though, so I grabbed my box and took it into my mom and dad's room. They weren't there, so I emptied the box on the bed. Taylor and I counted the Kisses and Hugs, and only two pieces were missing altogether. TWO HUGS! My favorites, that I'd been SAVING! My mom had eaten one and my dad had eaten the other.

"Emma didn't take ANY," Taylor said.

"Let's check the bed," I said, pulling Taylor by the arm.

Emma had left my room by then. We threw the blanket off the bed. The tape was not broken. We lifted the mattress. The disk was still there.

We went to look for my parents.

We found them at the front door, talking to Taylor's dad.

"Taylor, did you throw a crab apple at Billy's nose?" her dad asked her.

We both giggled, which wasn't really the best thing to do, I guess.

Her dad made her go home.

"Lucy, were you two being mean to Billy?" Mom asked.

"He's going to be our neighbor, so we need to be welcoming," Dad said.

Oh, brother, I thought.

"I thought you liked Billy," Mom said.

GEEZ, where had she been????

"It's not nice to hurt people," Dad said.

"And it's not nice to steal other people's candy," I said.

My mom and dad looked at each other and giggled.

(They can be SO childish when they're together.)

"How did you know?" Mom asked. Then she looked at the binoculars around my neck. "Oh, very clever," she said. "You were up in the crab apple tree, weren't you?"

"We're sorry," Dad said. "We thought you wouldn't mind sharing."

"Well, I do," I answered. "You might ask first."

"You're right," he said. "What can we do to make it up to you?"

That was a no-brainer.

"You can buy me a ferret," I said.

They laughed.

"We'll get you a new bag of candy — how 'bout that?" Dad said.

"Make it Hugs," I answered.

"And there's another baby box turtle at the nature center that someone found in the road. You could keep it in your room and feed it until we need to release it this fall," Mom offered.

"No thanks," I said.

Even though I REALLY like turtles, I HAD to hold out for the ferret.

"Well, sweetie, let me know if you change your

mind," Mom said. "I'm going to go help Grandma with the dishes."

"What's a contract?" I asked Dad.

"You mean, like on a house?" he asked me back.

"Yeah, Billy's parents put a contract on Mr. Owen's house," I told him.

"It means that Billy's parents have agreed to pay a certain price for the house," he said.

"So he'll be moving IN?" I asked, some panic in my voice, for sure.

"Probably, but first there has to be a closing, where there are lawyers and real estate people," he said.

"You mean there's NO chance he WON'T move in?" I asked. I really couldn't BELIEVE this was happening. What had I done to deserve this?

"Well, I wouldn't say that," Dad said. "Sometimes people change their minds before the settlement. In fact, that happened to us right before we bought this house. We had made an offer on another house, and then this one became available. We had to cancel that other contract."

"So what you're saying is that if Billy's parents find a house they like better, or find some reason they don't want to move into Mr. Owen's house, then they could cancel the contract?" I asked.

"Yes, I suppose, but it's a nice house, so I don't think that would happen," he said.

Hmm, I thought. There had to be *something* wrong with it.

"Isn't it a little small for his family?" I asked. "There are only two bedrooms, aren't there?"

"Well, there's the attic," Dad said. "They could make that another room if they need one."

I'd seen that attic before — very cobwebby and dark. "I don't think it would make a very good room," I said.

"Well, who knows what will happen," Dad said. "I'm sure there are at least a few more weeks before they close on the house."

So MAYBE there was time to work on this, I thought. I hoped!

"Do you think Taylor's dad will let me go over to see her?" I asked. I HAD to talk to her about this.

"Why don't you help me bake some brownies first? Maybe you could bring him one as a peace offering. Maybe you could find Billy and give him one, too," he said.

Brownies sounded like a great idea.

Giving one to Billy?

Oh, RIGHT.

I followed Dad into the kitchen, where Grandma was drying the dishes that Mom washed.

46

"Hello, dear, I haven't seen you in such a long time," Grandma said to me, all nice, like always. Which made me feel SO guilty for having yelled at her before.

"Hi, Grandma," I said.

"So, dear, how old are you now?" she asked me.

I felt like I would EXPLODE if I answered that question one more time!

"Lucy's ten," Dad said. "But just for a couple more months. Her birthday's in September."

I smiled at him for helping me out. Even though he had just been stealing my candy.

"Where have all the spoons gone?" my mom asked. "We used to have a whole set, and now I can only find two."

"Have you seen Pharaoh?" Grandma asked Dad. "I don't think he's had his supper."

"His name is MIL —" I started to say, but Dad gave me that "cut" sign. You know, when you slide your pointer finger along your neck and make a face?

He doesn't like us correcting Grandma. He says it's not respectful and it's silly, anyway, because she's just going to forget right away.

But — HELLO! — the cat's name is NOT Pharaoh! (I thought that REAL loud, but figured it was best not to really SAY it.)

47

Grandma opened a can of cat food and scooped it into a cat bowl with one of our two spoons, and then dropped the empty can AND the spoon into the trash can. Dad and I both saw her do it, and he reached into the trash and pulled it out, and started to say something to Grandma, but I gave him the "cut" sign. He laughed and dropped the spoon into the sink. Grandma hadn't noticed any of that, though. She was crumbling Ritz crackers over the lumps of food in Milky Way's bowl.

Dad and I made brownies, and I took one to Taylor's dad, who let me hang out with Taylor for exactly one hour. It wasn't enough time to come up with an actual plan to keep Billy off Oak Street, but we did come up with a name for the plan, if we ever can figure one out.

We're calling it "Operation ADIOS." ADIOS stands for: Annoying Doofus Invades Oak Street. (It wasn't easy coming up with the words to fit that.)

AnD tHat'S The eNd of tHe StOrY of A sTuPiD, StUpiD dAy.

I've got mail! I changed the songs, and now I hear the Beatles when I have mail. "Twist and Shout" is playing right now. I love that song! I think I'm going to have a Beatles dance party for my birthday in September. That would be fun. I better see who's

E-mailing me. Maybe it's Taylor and she's got some ideas for Operation ADIOS. . . .

‖ ‖ ‖ ‖ ‖ ‖ ‖ ‖ ‖ ‖ ‖ ‖ ‖ ‖ ‖ ‖ ‖ ‖ ‖ ‖

Subj: Your new neighbor
Date: 07/01/01 10:46:10pm Eastern Daylight Time
From: Darth
To: LucyLaLa

Lucy-Goosey,
I can't wait to be your next-door neighbor! Ha! Ha!
Bill

‖ ‖ ‖ ‖ ‖ ‖ ‖ ‖ ‖ ‖ ‖ ‖ ‖ ‖ ‖ ‖ ‖ ‖ ‖ ‖

I am NOT answering that! How annoying!
What a STUPID, stupid day!!!!

:-o

49

July 6, Thursday

Today I am going to use a new font. . . . And this will be it. Maybe it will help me to be in a cheerier mood. MAYBE it will help my feet feel better!

You see, on the Fourth of July, my mom got this big idea about going on a family hike into Washington, D.C. "We don't live very far away," she said. And I believed her. You see, we go into Washington sometimes, to the museums and all, and it isn't very far away. By SUBWAY. Or CAR.

So — since we BELIEVED Mom — Dad and Emma and I decided we would go with her. Meghan said she'd rather be with her friends, so she didn't go, and Grandma went with Norka to a picnic and fireworks.

50

Our goal was to get to the Washington
Monument, eat hot dogs, listen to the bands
(some old-people stuff), watch the fireworks,
and then take the subway home. It sounded
FINE. It didn't sound like it would KILL us. We
were all in good shape, Mom said. We would
have no problem walking that short distance.

Well, the Washington Monument is seven
miles away. It was 95 degrees outside. And
when we got there, we had to STAND in line
for hot dogs in a huge crowd of people from all
over the world. (I thought I was having heatstroke at one point, and that was why I
couldn't understand what the people next to
me were saying, but then Dad told me that
they were speaking German.)

We couldn't find anywhere to sit, so we
stood to listen to the bands. Finally, for the
fireworks, we sort of got to sit, but it was so
crowded we couldn't really totally sit — we
were kind of crouched, still on our feet. (The
fireworks were incredibly AWESOME. I have
never seen so many different colors in the sky!
And the fireworks made all these pictures, like
the American flag and stars and a peace sign.
It was great!!!)

After the fireworks it took us TWO

HOURS to get to the subway stop, which was RIGHT NEXT TO THE MONUMENT!! There were SO many people. I was afraid of getting lost in the crowd and ending up with some other family from Romania or Italy or Japan, and I would be lost in the world FOREVER.

But somehow (and I don't know exactly how, because I fell asleep STANDING UP on the subway, leaning against my dad), we got home and I woke up yesterday morning in my bed. And when I tried to get up, thinking it was any normal morning, I SCREAMED in PAIN! My legs hurt SO much I couldn't MOVE them!!!! My dad had to come help me get out of bed, and when I stood up I screamed even louder, because my feet hurt, too!! And then I screamed even louder when I looked at my feet — they were a disgusting, blistering, bloody mess. Dad got me a basin and I soaked my poor feet for an hour, and then he put Band-Aids all over them. It took THIRTEEN Band-Aids — per foot — to cover all the blisters. I'm NOT making that up! I still have the Band-Aids on my feet to prove it. Just look! I'm like *The Mummy.*

All right. I admit it. Mom was right that I

should have worn sneakers instead of sandals. At least my feet weren't hot during the walk. Putting ANY kind of shoe on was a major compromise as far as I'm concerned. I wanted to go barefoot. (Of course, I might not have any FEET left if I'd done THAT.)

ANYWAY, my dad got me downstairs yesterday by carrying me, and he asked me to please stay downstairs until I could go up the stairs by myself. (See? He's worn out from the walk, too!) Well, there was no way I was getting back up yesterday, even though I really wanted to write in my E-Journal. I was stuck on the living room couch the ENTIRE day and the ENTIRE night. I had to get off the couch a few times, and I was actually crawling. It was pathetic!

When Grandma saw me crawling she thought I was pretending to be a cat, and she brought me a bowl of cat food mixed with Cheerios (WEIRD), talked to me like I was a cat, and scratched my head. She likes to play. Dad says it's part of her illness. It makes her act like a kid. It was fun at first, but she wanted to do that for HOURS. She never gets tired of doing something fun, because she doesn't realize she's been doing it for a long time already. She can forget stuff right after it happens. (Boy, it must be strange being Grandma.)

After a while I told her I was a ferret, not a cat. She didn't know what a ferret was, and I showed her pictures in my book. She said she'd like to have one, and I called out to Dad and told him that. He laughed. He suggested I read to Grandma from my ferret book, and so I did. And this is some of the new stuff I learned about ferrets:

❤Ferrets can live in cages and are happy doing that, but they need several hours of freedom each day. They need to be played with. (*No problema* — that's Spanish for "no problem.")

❤Ferrets need to be bathed one or two times a month. You can bathe them in the sink, with water and ferret shampoo. You're supposed to talk to them while you do it. It relaxes them. You dry them with a fluffy towel, and if it's cold, you can use a hair dryer set on LOW. You can also brush them. (That sounds like fun!)

♥ You have to clip a ferret's nails about once a month. You can get a special tool for this. You have to clean their ears with a cotton swab once a month, too. They also need their teeth cleaned sometimes. These chores are tricky, the book says, and maybe a veterinarian can do it. (Good idea.)

♥ Ferrets like treats to eat and should get them after playtime. They like cereal, cucumbers, raisins, and stuff like that. They aren't supposed to get any dairy products, candy, or cake.

♥ They like toys, of course! If you pull a toy on a string, they like to chase it. If you pull an egg carton around on a string, the ferret might sit on it and go for a ride! If you put a pair of blue jeans on the floor, they will crawl in and out of the legs. And they like cat toys. (We have those!)

The next section in the book was about diseases ferrets can get, and I told Grandma I would read it later. I was tired, and I wanted to eat some popcorn and watch a movie on TV. Grandma said she liked that idea, but Norka came over then, and Dad suggested that she and Grandma might like to go to the animal shelter to see all the cats. I told Grandma to check and see if they had any ferrets at the animal shelter. I don't think she remembered, though, because when she got home she hugged me and told me I'd grown so much since the last time she'd seen me.

Oh, well.

Today I'm still in a lot of pain, but no one is helping me anymore. I'm hobbling around and moaning, but everyone thinks I'm just faking it, I think, because no one offers to get me anything or carry me anywhere. Maybe when Meghan gets up she'll help me. She's trying to be extra good because she kind of had a party at our house on the Fourth of July while we were in D.C. When we left that morning, she had a couple of friends here, and, well, some others came, I guess. Judging by the emptiness of the refrigerator and how sticky the floors were, and all the trash bags outside the back door, and — oh, yeah — the broken coffee table (it was made of GLASS), it might have been fifty people. Maybe more. Mom and Dad weren't real happy, and they told her she's grounded for the rest of her life. (I hope they were exaggerating.) Meghan's trying to be real helpful around the house so they'll change their minds.

I know I'd put in a good word for her if she'd get me food today. I'll cross my fingers that she'll come and ask me if I'm hungry. In the meantime, I'll just stay in front of this computer with my feet up, grab a circ-board, and catch a cyberwave!

BBS

Guess what? Meghan just appeared at my door to see if I need anything. YES!!! I asked for an ice cream sundae. I didn't have to tell her how to fix it, because she knows just how I like it. (EVERYONE in my family knows the ONLY way I eat ice cream sundaes is with crumbled chocolate chip cookies and a flood of chocolate syrup!) I can't wait to eat it!

You know where I just surfed to? I'll give you three guesses. YES! You got it on the first one (didn't you?)! The ferret site! I looked at some (I need a new word. . . . Let me look up "precious" in the thesaurus. . . .) DARLING pictures of ferrets. I've got them in a window here, and I'm going to stare at them until Meghan comes back with my sundae.

She's back!!!! I'm so glad! YUM!!!! There's so much chocolate syrup on the crumbled cookies and ice cream that I can't see anything under it!!! PERFECT! Meghan gave me a fork with it, though, and that's kind of weird. She said we don't have spoons anymore.

Bye!

G2G!

:-)

July 10, Monday

Today I went to work with Mom, which I ONLY do when I'm totally bored. Mom works at a nature center and takes care of lots of animals. She's called a "naturalist." Did you know that in England, people who don't wear clothes are called "naturists"? It sounds a lot like "naturalist," doesn't it? (My dad told us that. He knows about LOTS of words. Have I told you he's an English teacher?) I sure hope that people from England who meet my mom don't think she's a person who goes around with no clothes on. Eek!

My mom gets to wear jeans and a T-shirt to work. She also wears hiking boots and a khaki cap with her hair sticking out the hole in the back. (Mom and Emma have long, straight, light brown hair, and Meghan and I have shorter, wavy, blond hair. Dad has dark brown and gray curly hair.)

My mom's T-shirt and hat have the name of the nature center on them – "Nature's Nest." The words are made out of snakes, which always makes me think of the Slytherins in the Harry Potter books, because their symbol on the Hogwarts crest is a snake. I'd like it much better if there were lions on Mom's work clothes, like the Gryffindor symbol, but there aren't any lions at the nature center, so I guess that wouldn't make much sense. I don't really like snakes very much, but my mom sure does. She puts them around her neck and lets them squeeze her arm when she does programs, and she shows real long and scary snakes to people – mostly little kids. And they all think she's very brave.

But guess what? She's not really very brave at all. She's afraid to go on roller coasters, and I even had to hold her hand when we walked to the top of the Cape May Lighthouse last year. She also doesn't like really long and high bridges, like the Bay Bridge, which is three miles across the Chesapeake Bay and is REALLY cool. She has to close her eyes when Dad drives us across it each year on our way to the beach. Of course, that isn't happening this year. We aren't going to the beach. That was just one of the many complaints I decided to bring up while my mom drove us to the nature center this morning.

I was sitting in the front seat so I could talk to her, and because it's harder to sit in the back. It's filled up all the time with gardening stuff and bug catchers and pond nets, and it's a MESS. She used to bother me about my room being kind of messy, and then one day I asked her why she got to keep her car messy and I didn't get to keep my room messy. She told me I had a good point, and that she wouldn't bother me about my room any-more. And she hasn't, either. I wish she'd been that un-derstanding about the complaints I had this morning. This is how it went:

"Mom, are we not going to the beach because you're afraid of the bridge?" I asked her.

"No, Lucy, it's because we just need to spend less money this summer since we had all that work done in our yard to make a patio for Grandma," she an-swered.

"If we don't have enough money to pay for the beach trip, then how come we have enough money to pay for camp?" I asked.

Maybe she hadn't thought of that, I was hoping, and MAYBE, now that I had raised this very good and logical point, she was going to say, "Oh, my goodness, I hadn't thought of that. Of course we can't send you to camp! Do you mind if you miss camp, Lucy?"

But that's not what she said.

She said, "Camp doesn't cost as much as the beach,

and I think it's an important experience for kids. You're going to remember it for your whole life."

"Probably because I'll fall off a mountain and never walk again," I said. "Every time I turn the wheels of my wheelchair, I'll think of camp."

"I don't really think that will happen," she said. "You're just a little scared about going to overnight camp for the first time."

I decided to change the subject.

(Why do parents always make your very serious and complex feelings seem so SIMPLE?)

"Mom, I know you're going to think I'm not very nice for saying this," I said, "but it's WEIRD living with Grandma. She asks the SAME questions OVER AND OVER, all our spoons are missing, and she's always feeding poor Milky Way terrible things and calling him by the wrong name. It drives me CRAZY!"

"I know it's hard," Mom said. "But life isn't always filled with fun, and it's not always the way you plan. Grandma certainly didn't plan to have Alzheimer's disease. She can't live alone anymore, and I think it's just nicer for her to be with us instead of in a nursing home with a bunch of people she doesn't recognize. She wouldn't like that at all. It'll just take some time for you to get used to living with her."

"I don't think she recognizes me," I said. "She calls me 'dear.' She NEVER says my name."

"Maybe she doesn't remember your name, but I know she recognizes you," Mom said. "It'll be a nice break for you, getting away from all of us and going to camp, don't you think?"

I wanted to say, "Yeah, right," at that point, in a very sarcastic way. But I knew that wouldn't go over real big with Mom, so I decided to change the subject again.

"Mom, you HAVE to tell Billy's parents not to buy Mr. Owen's house," I said. "If Billy moves in next door, I'll be MISERABLE!"

"I thought you liked Billy," she said.

I couldn't BELIEVE she was still stuck on THAT idea!

"Mom, that's SO over," I said.

"Doesn't Taylor like Billy?" she asked.

(Does she pay ANY attention to what's going on in the world?!?)

"Taylor stopped liking Billy MONTHS ago," I told her.

"Billy's parents seem very nice," she said. "I'm looking forward to getting to know his mom. And Billy seems okay to me."

"But Billy isn't okay," I said, trying very hard to keep my tone NICE. "Have you forgotten what he did last year?"

She looked clueless. I couldn't BELIEVE it!

"You know! In the garden!" I said.

I couldn't believe she didn't remember what he had done. And she calls herself a NATURALIST!

It was so awful. It was a tragedy. It had to do with . . .

cAtERpiLLaR mUrDEr

In the spring, I had a real hard time picking a science project. Mom finally agreed to help me, and she told me that there were plants in her butterfly garden that are called host plants. Butterflies lay their eggs on the plants, because the caterpillars that come out of the eggs need these certain leaves to eat. Mom told me to keep my eye on the dill plants and make observations every day.

I watched the plants a lot, and kept a record of what was going on. There were these very big and beautiful, yellow-and-black-striped butterflies that came to the plants all the time. I looked them up in a book and found out they were swallowtails. And I read that they lay teeny-tiny yellow, pearly-looking eggs, and one day I actually found one of those on a dill plant. It was the size of the dot on this "i"! I'm not making this up!

After a few days, an itty-bitty baby caterpillar came out of the egg. It stayed on the plant and ate leaves, and it grew and grew. It got these real neat, wrinkly black and white and green stripes, and it did this awesome thing when I touched it — it shot out orange horns! I loved that caterpillar! I named it Dill, since that was its favorite food. Anyway, it got to be 3 centimeters and 9 millimeters long — I knew this because I measured it all the time — and then BILLY appeared in my yard one day.

I didn't see him at first, because I was busy measuring the caterpillar, and he sneaked up behind me and called me — oh, that horrible name! — Lucy-Goosey! And then he reached down and grabbed the caterpillar off the dill plant and SMOOSHED it. Green goop squirted out all over his hand, which made him yell — because he is SUCH a wimp — and then he reached out and wiped his hand IN MY HAIR!!!

I wanted to cry so badly, but I held my tears inside until I got into the house, and then I washed the slime that was once my little caterpillar friend out of my hair and shut the door of my room and stayed there for a really long time. I told Mom about it when she got home from work, and she helped me find another egg on the dill plants and I started my project over.

ThE eNd of tHAt
(aNd NoW i'D LiKE tO FoRgEt aLL AbOuT it, tHaNk YoU vErY mUcH)

Back to the car now . . .

"Oh, yes," Mom said. "The caterpillar episode. Well, it was only that once, wasn't it?"

"It was only MY caterpillar!" I said. My tone was definitely getting whiney, and I knew that wasn't a good thing. But I couldn't help it!

"Lucy, I can't control who buys Mr. Owen's house,"

Mom said. "Getting away at camp will make you forget about all that, won't it?"

I felt like I was going to shoot right out through the roof of the car, like one of those popper toys with the spring and the suction cup. HOW COULD SHE TURN EVERYTHING WE TALKED ABOUT INTO A QUESTION ABOUT CAMP?

Suddenly I noticed that Mom was pulling into the parking lot of the nature center. I quickly got to the point I'd been planning to make from the time I got into the car.

"Mom, it would be SO much easier to deal with all these ANNOYING things if I had a ferret," I said. And, yes, I really was whining now. So what! "You LOVE animals, Mom, so why can't we get one?"

"We've got so many animals now, and we're all adjusting to Grandma being with us. It's just not a good time," she said.

"It would help me adjust to Grandma if I had a ferret," I said. "And we wouldn't have so many animals if you didn't bring so many home all the time!"

"You're right, I know," she said. "I'll stop doing that, okay? And we'll talk again about the ferret idea next year. How about that?"

"Next YEAR?" I said. I felt tears trying to come, and part of me knew that Mom would feel more sorry for me if I let the tears go, but a stronger part of me held them back.

I got out of the car and sort of slammed the door. Mom made me open it again and shut it the right way.

Mom had to get ready for a reptile program right away, and I watched her take this very big black snake out of a tank in the middle of the nature center and put it around her neck. I followed her to the amphitheater in the woods, where there were, like, fifty little kids and their parents sitting around waiting for her to teach them about reptiles. I didn't stay to watch. I went down to the pond.

The pond is not real big, but it's real pretty. It has a bench that's perfect for sitting on while you write poetry. Which is what I like to do when I visit the nature center. Which is what I had brought my paper and pen for.

In school this year, Ms. P. really, really liked my poetry. (I HOPE HOPE HOPE I get a teacher next year who likes my poetry!) Ms. P. told me I was an excellent writer, and she told me I should write books when I grow up. Of course, I told her I was going to be a ferret breeder, but maybe I would find time to write a book about ferrets. A poetry book about ferrets would be something totally new, I bet. But I can only write poetry about things I see, or hear, or feel. I can't write about ferrets because I don't have one.

Well, anyway, I sat there on the bench at the pond, my pad of paper (black paper) and pen (silvery-green Milky Pen) ready. A great blue heron was standing in the water on the other side of the pond, like a statue. Turtles were lined up on a big log in the water. Dragonflies were sparkling like flying diamonds all over the place, and cicadas were making summery noises in the trees all around. Some little kids were on the dock dipping nets in the water — trying to get tadpoles, probably. I liked the whole scene. Here's the poem I wrote:

PoNd PoEtrY pLuS a WiSh

Dragonflies silently dart and dive
While buzzing cicadas sing and hide.
The turtles and heron are quiet and still,
Not moving a leg or eye or bill.
Could they dive in the pond or fly away
If someone or something scares them today?
A boy leans way over with his net
To reach a spot that's deep and wet,
But, uh-oh! Into the pond he crashes!
He and his net make two big splashes!
The turtles all dive and disappear

As the heron comes to life in fear!
Slowly it spreads its amazing wings
That make me think of dragons and kings,
And as I watch it turn to the sky,
Out of the pond steps the little guy,
All covered in muck and looking silly.
Boy, I wish that would happen to Billy.

‹S›

Mom was only working a half-day today, because she had some shopping to do. Before we left the nature center, I asked her if I could borrow some big bones. I was beginning to get an idea for Operation ADIOS, and I thought bones would come in handy. (I didn't tell her that, though.) She gave me some deer bones and told me how glad she was that I was getting interested in anatomy, and that I would probably see a lot of deer at camp.

(Argghh!)

Oh, well.

Today I changed my E-mail address. Since I've been getting E-mail from some people I don't like – like BILLY, for instance – I haven't used the Instant Messaging yet. I don't want Billy to start sending me messages all the time whenever I'm on-line. So I figured if I make a new E-mail address, and give it ONLY to people I can trust, then I won't have to worry about SOME people getting it.

My new E-mail address is FERRETLOVER@LEJ.COM.

I've got mail! Just when I was talking about my new E-mail address! Freaky! You know what song I've got playing now for my E-mail message? " HELP!" I LOVE that song. It's also very appropriate for the mail I think I'm getting right now. I E-mailed Aunt Katey this morning in New York. I asked her to PLEASE, PLEASE HELP ME by getting my mom to let me stay home instead of making me go to camp. I told her about how the hike on the Fourth of July almost KILLED me, and that for sure I couldn't make it through some wilderness thing! Mom listens to her because Aunt Katey's her older sister. It might be my only chance!

BRB

Subj: re: Camp
Date: 07/10/01 02:14:31pm Eastern Daylight Time
From: dziner
To: FERRETLOVER

DEAR LUCY,

IT'S SO GOOD TO HEAR FROM YOU! HOW DO YOU LIKE THAT E-JOURNAL? IT'S THE LATEST THING IN NEW

YORK. THE GIRL WHO LIVES IN THE APARTMENT NEXT DOOR SAYS SHE JUST GOT ONE. MAYBE YOU TWO COULD BECOME PEN PALS. BUT IF YOU'RE PALS ON E-MAIL, YOU DON'T USE PENS, DO YOU? SO WHAT WOULD YOU BE? E-PALS?

SO, YOU DON'T WANT TO GO TO CAMP? I'VE NEVER BEEN THE OUTDOORSY TYPE, EITHER. YOUR MOM WAS ALWAYS THE ONE COLLECTING THE ANIMALS AND HANGING AROUND AT THE CREEK, WHILE I WAS BUSY TALKING ON THE PHONE AND PAINTING MY NAILS. BUT I DID GO TO CAMP A FEW TIMES, AND I LIKED IT. THEY LET ME BRING MY NAIL POLISH, I REMEMBER. IT WAS FUN KAYAKING AND SWIMMING AND STUFF. I MET SOME FUN PEOPLE. I'M STILL FRIENDS WITH SOMEONE I MET IN CAMP, AND SHE LIVES HERE IN NEW YORK CITY. WE DO LUNCH ONCE A MONTH. SHE'S AN ARTIST.

SORRY TO HEAR YOU WERE IN PAIN AFTER THE FOURTH. WALKING TO D.C.? NOW THAT'S A BIT MUCH, I'D SAY. OF COURSE, I WALK A LOT, SINCE I DON'T HAVE A CAR, BUT I TAKE A CAB OR THE SUBWAY WHEN I WANT TO GET TO GREENWICH VILLAGE OR THE THEATER DISTRICT. AND THAT'S A WHOLE LOT CLOSER THAN YOU ARE TO D.C.!

I'LL TALK TO YOUR MOM ABOUT THE CAMP. IT'S PROBABLY ALREADY PAID FOR, SO I DOUBT SHE'LL CHANGE HER MIND. MAYBE NEXT SUMMER YOU COULD COME UP HERE AND STAY WITH ME INSTEAD OF GOING

TO OVERNIGHT CAMP. WE HAVE LOTS OF GREAT DAY CAMPS HERE IN THE CITY — REAL ARTSY, YOU KNOW. THERE'S DRAMA, PAINTING, SCULPTURE, WRITING, AND OTHER HIP THINGS. YOU'D FIT RIGHT IN.

I'VE GOT TO GO. I'M AT WORK, YOU KNOW. I HAVE TO GET A DESIGN IN BY 4:00 TODAY, AND I'M NOT DONE!

LOVE TO ALL!

AUNT KT

Aunt Katey is very cool. She's a clothing designer. Sometimes she makes costumes for shows. I wish I WERE going to camp in New York City! If I live through summer camp this year, I'll work on Mom about letting me go up there. That sure sounds a lot better than marching around in the woods getting blisters.

|-o

July 12, Wednesday

Taylor is at her mother's house this week. Her mother doesn't live all that far away, but you can't walk there. (Unless you're my mom.) I called there yesterday, because I wanted to talk (like, real talk), which we haven't done all week. No one was home, though, so I left a message on the voice mail asking Taylor to IM me at exactly 12:00 noon today.

I also said in the message that she should try to find out when Billy is going to be at Mr. Owen's house again. I said I couldn't E-mail him because then he'd find out my new E-mail address and the whole point of changing it was because of him, and I didn't want anything to do with him anyway. (Taylor doesn't mind talking to him — she says it's fun to tease him.) At the end of my phone message, I said "¡ADIOS!"

That's my secret way of telling her we need to work on Operation ADIOS. We don't want any parents figuring out what we're up to, or they'll stop us for sure.

Oh! It's almost noon. 10-9-8-7-6-5 —

Yes! She's even 5 seconds early!

I know I have an IM because music plays, just like when I have E-mail. But I've programmed it for a different song — "(You Drive Me) Crazy!" I'll switch screens . . .

HIPHIPPIE: HEY LUCY! ZUP? I LOVE YUR NEW EMAIL ADDRESS!

FERRETLOVER: THANX! I'M NOT GIV-ING IT 2 N-E-1 YET, EXCEPT U. WELL, MY FAMILY KNOWS, TOO, BECAUSE I HAD 2 GET THEIR HELP SO I COULD CHANGE IT. N-E UPDATE ON OPERATION ADIOS?

HIPHIPPIE: YEP! I FOUND OUT WHAT WE NEED 2 KNOW. BILLY'S GOING 2

THE HOUSE ON MONDAY. HIS PARENTS
R MEETING SOME PEOPLE THERE, OR
SOMETHING. HE SAID HE CAN'T WAIT 2
C HIS NEW NEXT-DOOR NEIGHBOR
(YEAH, RIGHT!).

FERRETLOVER: OH, PLEEEEZE!!! CAN'T
WAIT 2 RUIN MY LIFE IS MORE LIKE IT.
ANYWAY, MONDAY'S PERFECT!!!! U'LL B
BACK BY THEN!!!! I WAS THINKING WE
COULD PUT BONES UP IN THE ATTIC 2
SCARE HIM.

HIPHIPPIE: HUMAN BONES? EEK!

FERRETLOVER: GROSS! NOT HUMAN
BONES! I'VE GOT DEER BONES — THEY
LOOK PRETTY HUMAN 2 ME, THOUGH!

HIPHIPPIE: WHERE DID U GET DEER
BONES?

FERRETLOVER: I WENT 2 WORK WITH
MOM N GOT THEM AT THE NATURE
CENTER. THAT'S HOW BORED I AM
WHEN U R AT YUR MOM'S!

HIPHIPPIE: SORRY! R U SURE WE SHOULD GO UP IN MR. OWEN'S ATTIC? THAT SOUNDS CREEPY 2 ME.

FERRETLOVER: TAYLOR, WE HAVE 2 KEEP BILLY OFF OAK STREET, DON'T WE? WE AREN'T GOING 2 DO THAT BY BE-ING WIMPY, LIKE HE IS. WE'VE GOT TO SAY "ADIOS" TO BILLY, DON'T WE?

HIPHIPPIE: I GUESS U R RIGHT. BUT HOW DO WE GET IN THE HOUSE?

FERRETLOVER: I THOUGHT OF THAT AL-READY. WE HAVE A KEY 2 HIS BACK DOOR. MR. OWEN GAVE IT 2 US A LONG TIME AGO, SO WE COULD FEED HIS DOG N STUFF WHEN HE WAS AWAY. HE TOLD ME I WAS WELCOME 2 VISIT N-E-TIME. AND EVEN THOUGH HE'S NOT AROUND N-E-MORE, WELL, IT'S STILL HIS HOUSE, TECHNICALLY, ISN'T IT?

HIPHIPPIE: I GUESS.

FERRETLOVER: MAYBE WE COULD SLOP BLOOD ALL OVER THE BONES 2 MAKE THEM LOOK EVEN SCARIER.

HIPHIPPIE: BLOOD? YUCK!

FERRETLOVER: NOT REAL BLOOD. KETCHUP MAYBE?

HIPHIPPIE: OR STRAWBERRY JAM?

FERRETLOVER: DISGUSTING N EXCELLENT! THAT'S GLOPPIER. <S>

HIPHIPPIE: HOW R WE GOING 2 GET BILLY 2 GO UP IN THE ATTIC?

FERRETLOVER: I DON'T KNOW . . .

HIPHIPPIE: I'LL DARE HIM. THAT ALWAYS WORKS.

FERRETLOVER: IT WOULD B COOL 2 GET MILKY WAY UP THERE, TOO! WE CAN LURE HIM UP WITH A BOWL OF FOOD N THEN MAYBE HE'LL STAY THERE LONG ENOUGH 4 BILLY 2 SEE HIM. THAT'LL FREAK HIM OUT! HE'S AFRAID OF MILKY WAY!

HIPHIPPIE: G2G! MOM N I R GOING SHOPPING. I'LL PICK UP THE JAM TODAY. EMAIL ME L8R! ADIOS!

FERRETLOVER: ADIOS!!!

Okeday! This is going to be great! We'll sneak some bones up to the attic on Monday, glop some red jam all over them, lure the cat up there, and then make sure Billy just happens to go in there. That should totally freak him out. He'll beg his parents not to move in. I hope!!!

I've got E-mail! I better check and see who it is. . . .

Subj: Important Message
Date: 07/12/01 12:14:21pm Eastern Daylight Time
From: FUSVJ
To: FERRETLOVER

Modz Hiitaz,

E dup'v xuev vi ca zios pax paehjcis!

Cemm

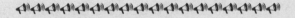

Wow! How weird is that? I know it's not Pig Latin.

Who would send something totally bizarre like that? And what kind of E-mail address is "FUSVJ," anyway? Maybe it's supposed to say something, like the net-yak we use. But what? It doesn't even get close to saying anything. At least not in English. Hey! Maybe it's Russian! Maybe it's from a spy, or someone cool like that! But why would a spy send something to me? Well . . . maybe there's a spy out there with a screen name like mine, and this was sent to me by accident. But, ya know, I really don't think a person like a spy would have a screen name anything like FERRETLOVER. Do you?

I wish I could E-mail a reply, but I'm not al-

79

lowed to talk with anyone on the Internet I don't know. Mom says if she discovers that any of us do that, she won't let us use the Internet anymore. That would be awful!!! There's no way I'd risk that! After all, it could be her sending the E-mail to try to test me. Doesn't sound like something she'd do, though.

But . . . wait a minute! It does sound like something Emma would do. And she does know how to change her E-mail address — I know that because she helped me change mine. Come to think of it, she was awfully nice about helping me. Maybe she only helped me so she could find out my E-mail address, so she could send this bizarre E-mail to me, which she knew would drive me crazy. Maybe she is hoping I will answer it and then she can get me in trouble, so she will have more time on the computer! Or even get the computer moved to her room! She has been pretty jealous about it being in here and all. . . .

I think I'll find Dad and tell him all about it. TTFN

Well, I showed the message to Dad. He said it looks like a code of some sort, and he said he was on his way to the library, anyway, and he'd see if there were any books on codes.

Dad is very into the library. He goes, like, every day. He's a book-crazed man! Yesterday he made Meghan go with him, because she has this really long list of books she's supposed to read this summer and she hasn't even read one word of anything yet. (Except teen magazines, I think — there are ads from teen magazines covering the walls of her room and covering the ceiling, too. She uses a staple gun to put them up, and when she's decorating, it sounds like Woody Woodpecker is on our roof.) Anyway, yesterday they came back from the library with this huge stack of books, which Meghan said she couldn't carry up into her room, so Dad took some of them up for her. I don't think she's started reading any. Dad asks her, though, every time he sees her, and it makes her real mad. It goes sort of like this. . . .

MEGHAN: What's for dinner, Dad?

DAD: We're having the same thing that Huck and Tom had in Chapter 37 of *The Adventures of Huckleberry Finn.*

MEGHAN: DAD! What are we having for
dinner?

I showed the mystery E-mail to Norka, too. I
figured since she knows at least one more language than I do, she would have some ideas. I
found her in the kitchen with Grandma and Milky
Way, who was rubbing back and forth against
Grandma's legs. Grandma was breaking a chocolate bar into little pieces over a dish of cat food.
When she was done, she set it on the floor in
front of him and he actually ate the glop —
chocolate and all! Which made me kind of annoyed, because I know it's not good for cats to
eat stuff like that. It also made me annoyed that
Milky Way's jingly bell collar was clanging against
the cat dish as he ate, reminding me of Billy,
since he was the one who put the collar on him in
the first place. I thought to myself, "Why are we
keeping that bell on the cat, anyway?" and I
reached down and unhooked it (which didn't disturb Milky Way's eating at all) and I threw it in the
trash. That made me feel a whole lot better. And
then I asked Norka if she would look at the E-mail
for me.

She didn't understand it, either, but she said
there was a Latin word in it — *pax*. It means

"peace," she said. But the other words weren't Latin, she didn't think. So I don't know if that's a clue or not. I asked her if she thought it might be some kind of code, and she said she didn't know, and that she and Grandma had to get going, because they were due at the animal shelter. She said that Grandma is an official volunteer there now. Which is pretty cool, I think. So I asked Grandma what she does as a volunteer there, but she didn't know what I was talking about.

"Your grandmother's job is to sit with the cats and pet them and talk to them for an hour each day, Tuesday through Friday," Norka told me.

"Are there ferrets at the shelter?" I asked.

"Parrots?" Grandma said. "I'd like one of those."

"No, Grandma, please don't get a parrot," I said to her. I knew we'd never get a ferret if we got any more new pets!

I ran into the living room to find my ferret book so I could show Grandma a picture of a ferret, but I couldn't find it anywhere. (Even though I know I left it on the coffee table.)

I tried to explain to Grandma what a ferret looks like — cute and fuzzy, cute and long, cute and adorable. But she got distracted by Milky

Way, who was rubbing up against her legs again. Boy, he can eat fast!

"Has Pharaoh had supper?" Grandma asked.

"Yes!" I said. I know I sounded a little impatient. But, geez! That cat's going to bust one of these days! I can just see it — cat food, chocolate, guts, and hair flying all over the house! Gross!

Oh! I've got another E-mail. Maybe it's an ADIOS update from Taylor. . . .

•• •• •• •• •• •• •• •• •• •• •• •• •• •• •• •• •• ••

Subj: Another Important Message
Date: 07/12/01 01:18:15pm Eastern Daylight Time
From: FUSVJ
To: FERRETLOVER

Modz Hiitaz,

E dup'v xuev opvem Nipfuz!

Cemm

🗨🗨🗨🗨🗨🗨🗨🗨🗨🗨🗨🗨🗨🗨🗨🗨

I can't believe this!!! Another one! And Emma's not home, which means she could be sending this from a friend's house.

Hmm . . . I think I agree with my dad that it's a code, because there are some words that are completely the same as the last E-mail. I'm going to paste both messages next to each other here:

Modz Hiitaz,
E dup'v xuev vi ca zios pax paehjcis!
Cemm

and . . .

Modz Hiitaz,
E dup'v xuev opvem Nipfuz!
Cemm

What in the world is a Nipfuz?

"Modz Hiitaz" must be a greeting, because it's the same in both messages, and it has a comma after it and all. Maybe "Modz" means "Dear." But what about "Hiitaz"? There are too many letters for it to mean "Lucy." The next line in each message starts with "E dup'v xuev." "E" might mean "I" or "A" because those are the only two letters that are words all by themselves. The last word,

"Cemm," must be a name. A name! A name with "emm" in it! More proof that it could be Emma!

I just remembered! Last year at the school book fair, Emma bought this book about notes. Mostly it told about folding notes, but there were some codes in it, too! (I sort of borrowed it once, and Emma had a fit when she couldn't find it one day. I couldn't find it, either, and she got real mad. Dad found it under my bed — I don't know how it got there!) I wonder where that book is? I would check in her room right now, but I just heard her come in the front door. (I know it's her because I can hear a basketball bouncing on the stairs.) I know! I'll tell her she can have a turn on the computer, and I'll sneak into her room while she's in here. Wish me luck!

BBL!

I'm writing before bed. I'm too tired to write about how I made a fool of myself in front of Emma today. Anyway, I already explained it to Taylor in an E-mail, so I'll just paste a copy of it here:

YKW? I've been getting these very weird E-mails. They're
either total nonsense (2 drive me crazy) or they're in code.
I think Emma's doing it. How can my parents even
THINK about sending me 2 camp with someone like
THAT???!!!

Emma has a code book, but she won't let me C it. I asked
her about it today, N she SAYS it's LOST. RIGHT!!! I tried 2
sneak into her room 2 look 4 it. She was using the computer in my room, N I stomped downstairs (real loud, so
she would hear me go down), N then I quietly crept back
upstairs (like a cat, so she wouldn't hear me go up), then I
silently slithered back by the door of my room (on the floor,
like a gecko, so she wouldn't C me), then I stood up slowly
in front of her door (which was closed), N I turned the knob,
N U KNOW WHAT? AN ALARM WENT OFF!!!

WHEN DID EMMA GET A DOOR ALARM???

I'll figure out a way 2 catch her, though. It HAS 2 B her.
Did U get the jam?

ADIOS,
Lucy

~:-o

July 13, Thursday

Remember how I couldn't find my ferret book yesterday? Well, that's because it was in . . . the trash can! Can you believe that? Today Meghan was emptying the trash (still trying to get my parents to unground her), and she noticed a pair of reading glasses (Dad's), a candle, a deck of cards, two magazines, and MY BOOK in there, covered with coffee grounds and mayonnaise and other disgusting things that I don't want to talk about.

Do you know how all that stuff got in the trash? Dad says Grandma must have thrown it away by ACCIDENT, trying to clean up! It was all stuff that was on top of the coffee table.

MY POOR FERRET BOOK!

It was all covered with gross stuff, and Dad tried to wash it in the sink but the pages just started falling apart. I told him to forget it.

He said we should keep our valuable stuff upstairs in our rooms, since Grandma doesn't go upstairs because of her right knee, which hurts sometimes, so I went all around and gathered up all the games and things I have ALWAYS kept downstairs, and I dragged it all up to my room. My room is getting so crowded! My LIFE is getting so crowded!

Funny thing, though . . . while I was running around down there, getting all my stuff, Meghan showed up in the living room with all the books she's supposed to read this summer, and she plopped them down on the coffee table and left.

(I really don't think that's going to work.)

Oh! I've got mail. I HOPE it's Taylor! PLEASE PLEASE PLEASE BE TAYLOR!

꒹ ꒹ ꒹ ꒹ ꒹ ꒹ ꒹ ꒹ ꒹ ꒹ ꒹ ꒹ ꒹ ꒹ ꒹ ꒹ ꒹ ꒹ ꒹

Subj: Important Message
Date: 07/13/01 11:42:41 Eastern Daylight Time
From: FUSVJ
To: FERRETLOVER

Modz Hiitaz,

Zio Ipix xji huwa na zios A-nuem uffsatt? Zios catv gseapf,
Vuzmis!

Cemm

AAHHHHH!!!!
I'm SO CLUELESS I CAN'T STAND IT! And I
STILL haven't been able to get that code book
from Emma. She STILL pretends she doesn't
know where it is, and she shuts her door every
time she leaves her room, which means the
alarm is probably on. I guess I'll get Dad to
look at this E-mail. He got some books at the
library yesterday, which he has been reading
ever since he got home. (WHAT a book-crazed
man!) The books he got seem to be all
about the CIA and spies and stuff, and I don't
see what all that has to do with cracking an
E-mail code, but I'll try him anyway. I'm pretty
desperate.
BBS

****

Dad looked at the message for a long time. He said it's definitely not Navajo. I don't know what that has to do with anything, which should give you some idea of how much help he was. He did say, though, that it's pretty clear that each letter translates to another letter. He agrees that "Cemm" is probably the name of the person who is sending them, since it has appeared in all three messages. I told him I am suspicious of Emma, since it has one "e" and two "m"s in it, and he said something like, "Oh, your sister wouldn't tease you like that."

AS IF!

Then he asked me if I need a book to read, and I said, "Yes, as a matter of fact I need a children's book on notes and codes and stuff," and he said he did look at the library, but all the books like that were out. I told him Emma probably checked them all out and hid them. And I told him that she already owns a code book, but she won't let me borrow it, and he said he'd ask her about it.

Maybe that will work.

I'm going to copy the three E-mails together here. Maybe that will help. . . .

Modz Hiitaz,

E dup'v xuev vi ca zios pax paehjcis!

Cemm

and

Modz Hiitaz,

E dup'v xuev opvem Nipfuz!

Cemm

and

Modz Hiitaz,

Zio lpix xji huwa na zios A-nuem uffsatt? Zios catv gseapf, Vuzmis!

Cemm

WHAT is a Vuzmis???
HEY!!! It's the 21st century, isn't it? I bet there's a website for codes. I'm goin' surfin'!!!
BRB

ॐ ॐ ॐ ॐ ॐ ॐ ॐ ॐ ॐ ॐ ॐ ॐ ॐ ॐ ॐ ॐ ॐ ॐ ॐ

WWW.THUNK.COM!! What a fun website! It's got this message scrambler in it. You type a message into this box and then click on the "Scramble" button, and the letters all change around into something unreadable. You can write an E-mail message to someone, put it in the scrambler, and then the person you send it to can't read it until they go to the website and put the message into the descrambler. COOL!

There's also a page on the website that tells about the history of secret messages. It was pretty interesting to read about. Did you know that the first secret messages were sent over 2,000 years ago, and that Julius Caesar wrote to his friends in code? And during World War II, Native Americans helped our country make a secret code based on the Navajo language. (I guess that's what Dad was talking about.) And do you know what? Some kid in Ireland won a bunch of awards for inventing a new way to send secret E-mail! AWESOME!

One thing I didn't learn on the website was how to decode my mystery E-mails. I put them in the descrambler, but it only turned the nonsense words into different nonsense words. Bummer.

I'm going to search some more. . . .
BRB

꒡꒡꒡꒡꒡꒡꒡꒡꒡꒡꒡꒡꒡꒡꒡꒡꒡꒡꒡꒡

I couldn't find any other code sites, so I did a
Yahooligans search (you know, WWW.
YAHOOLIGANS.COM) for some information
about Alzheimer's disease. My dad keeps asking
me to do that, and now I've done it. The
Alzheimer's websites are really boring. There are
no animals running around the screen, and no
colors. They come from medical places, so all the
words are real big. There was only one that I
could understand, and this is what I learned:

Alzheimer's disease means your brain is getting sort of eaten up somehow. There are seven
stages of the disease, and stage seven is so awful I don't want to talk about it. I'd say Grandma is
in stage five. That means she doesn't recognize
people very well, needs help with lots of things,
and can't remember too much.

But, you know, Grandma remembers some
stuff REALLY well. I know this because of what
happened the other night when we went out to
dinner. I think I'll write about it. I'll call this story . . .

ThE SpAgheTTysBuRg aDDrEss

We hadn't been out to dinner for a while, so we decided to go to one of our favorite places — the Prime Time Family Restaurant. We went at about 5:00 P.M., which is pretty early for dinner, and so there were NO people there at all when we first arrived. My mom said Grandma would get tired, so that was why we were eating so early.

I wanted to sit in this booth that we have ALWAYS sat in for as long as I can remember. It's in the corner, and sort of surrounded by statues, so we feel like it's totally private, and that's fun. But we couldn't sit there that night, and it's not because someone else was sitting there, it was because the booth isn't big enough for six people, which is the size of our family now that Grandma lives with us. So they sat us at this really long table in the VERY middle of the restaurant, which is totally the opposite of private. And that, I think, was the biggest mistake of the evening. Well, actually, the BIGGEST mistake might have been the way the waitress pronounced the word *spaghetti*.

"Saturday is pasketti night," she said in a very clear and loud voice. "All you can eat."

And, yes, she really DID say "pasketti." I know

96

that usually it's just little kids that say that, and I know that this waitress was at least a teenager, but that's what she said.

"It's pronounced 'spaghetti,' dear," Grandma said to the waitress.

Grandma used to be a teacher, and so she likes correcting people's words, at least when she can hear them. Dad says it drove him crazy when he was little, so I don't know WHY he became a teacher, too, but he did. (He corrects people's words, too.)

Anyway, the waitress smiled and filled up our water glasses and set down a basket of rolls in the middle of the table.

"So, do you all want the pasketti?" she asked.

"It's pronounced 'spaghetti,' dear," Grandma said again.

"That's what I said," the waitress said.

"No, you said 'pasketti,'" Grandma told her. "It's pronounced spa-ghet-ti."

I knew this could go on for a while, and so I put down my menu. I didn't need it anyway. I knew what I wanted — spaghetti, all I could eat. I was hungry. I took a roll out of the basket and ate it while I watched the door of the restaurant, which I could see from where I was sitting at the table. People were arriving now, and I recognized this one family that came in — the McCallisters. They have two kids — a son who plays baseball with Emma and a son who goes to college. But I guess he's home for the summer, because he was with them.

Meghan, I know, has a big crush on this college boy, but she hadn't noticed that he was in the restaurant, because she was across the table from me and couldn't see the door. And she was kind of distracted, anyway. She had joined in with the whole "pasketti" thing.

"This is a FREE COUNTRY," Meghan was saying. "People should be allowed to SAY things the way they WANT to!"

She was getting all upset and waving her arms in the air, and her voice was getting louder. She didn't notice when the McCallisters sat down at the table right next to us, or when the college boy sat in the seat RIGHT behind her. I leaned down a little and pointed my finger behind my hand, because I figured she might want to know, but she ignored me.

"We didn't go to war with England to have someone TELLING us how to pronounce our words —" she was saying, and it was right about that time that she noticed me mouthing the words

98

"Look behind you," and she glanced to her side and then did a major double take, and then she completely shut up. And she turned totally red and got up and headed in the direction of the rest rooms.

"Did you want the pasketti?" the waitress called after her.

"It's pronounced 'spaghetti,' dear," Grandma said.

Dad gave the waitress a look that said, "Go ahead and get her the spaghetti."

"Did you teach your students about the Revolutionary War, Mom?" Dad asked her. I know he was trying to change the subject.

The waitress looked at me, and I said, "I'd like the sp — special, please." And then she looked at Emma, who had just discovered her baseball friend at the nearby table (his name is PJ, and I have no idea what that stands for). They were both sitting at the ends of the tables, kind of sideways to each other, and were looking at each other out of the corner of their eyes, like they were out on the field and couldn't miss a play or something. She wasn't paying any attention when the waitress asked her what she wanted. Twice.

"What would you like, Emmy-bemmy?" Mom said to her.

(Why do parents DO that?)

PJ laughed and Emma rolled her eyes and said she'd have a hamburger and tater tots. Then my mom pointed to something she wanted on the menu, and while she was doing that the first roll flew over from the other table and hit Emma on the side of the head. Emma didn't really react much, she just grabbed a roll out of the basket on our table and chucked it right over, and it hit PJ in the head.

"The Revolutionary War . . ." Grandma was saying. "Hmm, no, I don't think so, I taught the Civil War, yes, that was it. I had my sixth graders memorize the Gettysburg Address. That was fun."

That didn't sound fun to me. That sounded hard.

"Emma, did you learn the Gettysburg Address this year?" Dad asked her.

A couple of rolls hit each other in midair just when Dad looked over, and he gave Emma a look that said, "You better stop that," and then she gave him a look that said, "Stop what?"

"Abraham Lincoln made that speech on the Gettysburg battlefield on November 19, 1863," Grandma said.

I was real surprised she remembered that.

And I was even more surprised when she started reciting it.

"Four score and seven years ago our fore-fathers brought forth on this continent, a new nation, conceived in Liberty . . ."

I can't remember the rest of it, but Grandma sure did. And she probably hadn't recited that thing since before I was born. She was using her best schoolteacher voice, too, and all this emotion, and she stood up and used her arms at important parts of the speech. And by the time she got to the end — the part that says "of the people, by the people, for the people," all the people in the restaurant had stopped what they were doing and were looking at her. She was THERE. She was GETTYSBURG. She wasn't even thrown off when a roll zipped through the air like a cannonball and hit her in the arm.

That's what was going on when Meghan opened the rest room door and stepped back into the restaurant. By the look on her face I'd say she wished she'd climbed out of the bathroom window instead. She looked at the table for less than one second, and then she walked directly out of the restaurant, like she didn't even know us. Mom went after her.

Everyone in the restaurant clapped when

Grandma was done, and she gave a little bow and sat down. The waitress was clapping, too, and she came over and refilled Grandma's water glass.

"I think we're ready to order," Grandma said to her. "Are there any specials tonight?"

aNd ThAt'S tHe EnD of ThAt!

Hey! "Crazy" is playing. You know what THAT means. I have an IM. . . .

☎ ☎ ☎ ☎ ☎ ☎ ☎ ☎ ☎ ☎ ☎ ☎ ☎ ☎ ☎ ☎

HIPHIPPIE: YKW? I'VE GOT THE STRAW-BERRY JAM.

FERRETLOVER: GR8! IS IT REAL GLOPPY?

HIPHIPPIE: I HOPE SO. I'M NOT OPEN-ING IT UNTIL MONDAY.

FERRETLOVER: U WON'T BELIEVE THIS! I GOT ANOTHER ONE OF THOSE E-MAILS!

HIPHIPPIE: NW!

FERRETLOVER: DO U KNOW N-E-THING ABOUT CODES?

HIPHIPPIE: NO.

FERRETLOVER: IT'S EITHER EMMA DOING IT OR ELSE SHE GAVE MY E-MAIL ADDRESS 2 SOMEONE ELSE WHO'S SENDING THEM. SHE'S THE ONLY ONE WHO WOULD DO SOME-THING LIKE THAT.

FERRETLOVER: HEY! N-E-1 THERE? I'VE BEEN WAITING LIKE A WHOLE MINUTE HERE.

HIPHIPPIE: SORRY! GOT DIS-TRACTED! G2G.

Two more days till Taylor gets back. It seems like a million years. She'll help me figure out this

E-mail thing, AND we'll be able to rid Oak Street of Billy once and for all! Taylor and I RULE!
  ADIOS!

  ]|:-)

July 24, Monday

Well, it's been over a week since my last entry, E-Journal. After what happened last Monday, my parents told me I couldn't get on the computer for a whole week. I was BEACHED! You know, like a whale out of water. No E-Journal, no E-mail, no IMs, no surfing for a week! I spent a whole lot more time riding my bike up and down the driveway and going to the nature center with Mom, I'll tell you that. I couldn't even work on cracking the E-mail code because I couldn't get on the computer to see the messages! I'd printed out some copies before, but I just couldn't find any of those around the house. Maybe Grandma threw them away. Or Emma!

Speaking of E-mails, when I logged on today, there were a bunch of them in my mailbox. Mostly they were from Taylor (who was allowed to be on the computer last week, but was GROUNDED and also couldn't use the phone, so I didn't get to make any contact with her ALL week), but her E-mails just said how bored she was. One was from Aunt Katey, just checking in to see how I was doing. She said it was 102 degrees in New York! Then there was one from guess who, that FUSVJ! I'll copy it into the E-Journal soon, because there are some codes I've learned about that I want to try out on the mystery E-mails. But first I need to tell you about what happened last Monday, and why I was beached.

By the way, my mom isn't mad at me anymore, even though I'd NEVER seen her as mad as she was that day. Well, it wasn't really ME she was most mad at. I did feel very bad about what happened and all. But it all ended up okeday. And it was SO funny. Maybe the funniest thing that's EVER happened. In the HISTORY of EVER. Definitely worth a week of being beached. (But don't tell my mom.)

I'll call this story . . .

ReVeNGe rOcKS!!

Last Monday, as planned, Taylor came over in the morning. She burst into my room, where I was trying to decide how to arrange the deer bones so they'd look like human bones, and she was ALL

stressed out. She'd brought this little jar of strawberry jam over to her dad's house with her on Saturday, she said, and she'd left it on the kitchen
counter.

MISTAKE! What was she thinking, leaving a key
ingredient to Operation ADIOS out in the open?

Turns out her dad LOVES strawberry jam, and he
thought it was there to eat. (Now WHY would he
think to eat jam that he sees on the kitchen
counter, I asked Taylor. I don't think she appreci-
ated my sarcasm.) He had jam on bagels, and on
toast, and on oatmeal, and on pizza (not really, I
was just making sure you're awake). So when she
went to get the jar on Monday morning, she found
it in the recycling bin, all rinsed out and ready for
the recycling truck.

It just so happened that Norka was taking my
grandma grocery shopping that day. Norka thought
it would be a good thing to do, since the animal
shelter is closed on Mondays. Dad had given her a
list of stuff to get, and they were going in the afternoon. I was sure they'd be happy to have our com-
pany, so I told Taylor everything would be all right.
Operation ADIOS would be a go, on schedule!

Taylor said Billy was supposed to show up at
Mr. Owen's house around 5:00 P.M., after his mom
and dad got off work. I figured that would give us

107

plenty of time. We could go into Mr. Owen's house and put the bones in the attic BEFORE we went to the store, and then when we had the jam, we would just add that, and take the cat up there then, too.

Good plan, we thought.

(Actually, it was more than a plan. I'm looking up the word *plan* in the thesaurus . . . here's a new word: SCHEME! Good SCHEME!)

So, anyway, we put the bones in a bag, got the key, and went in the back door of Mr. Owen's house and up the skinny, creaky stairs. Our shoes made sounds that echoed above and below us, like ghosts bouncing into walls, and we were both kind of getting the creeps. When we got to the attic door we just looked at it at first, and then I reached out and put my hand on the knob and twisted it. It squeaked, which made us jump, and when I pushed on it, it wouldn't open.

"Maybe there's a lock," Taylor whispered.

"No, I don't see one," I whispered back. "The doors in my house just stick sometimes, and maybe this one hasn't been opened in a while."

"Yeah, the doors stick in my house, too," Taylor whispered.

"Why are we whispering?" I asked, and then laughed.

Taylor laughed, too. We laughed loud, and I

pushed real hard on the door, and it flew open with a BANG! And then THINGS started flying around in the dark in there, and we SCREAMED, and I threw the bag of bones through the door and we ran down the stairs, the echoey sounds of our shoes chasing us all the way down and out the back door. We were panting and shaking. Then we looked at each other and started laughing again.

"Were they bats?" Taylor asked, breathing hard all around her laughs.

"I guess," I said, breathing hard, too. "Mom says bats won't hurt people."

"Don't they suck blood?" Taylor asked.

"Not the ones around here," I told her. "They eat insects at night, and they sleep during the day."

"They were sleeping up there?" Taylor asked.

"I guess," I said. "Mom gave us this whole lecture one night at dinner about bats, how people don't appreciate them, and how they eat hundreds of mosquitoes each night, and how they have no habitat around here. I think she'll be pleased to know they have a habitat in Mr. Owen's attic."

"What do we do now?" Taylor asked.

We'd gotten our breath back by then, and I wasn't feeling scared anymore. (Well, not REAL scared, anyway.)

"We're going back in," I said.

"Are you sure?" Taylor asked.

"We'll just move real slowly up there, so we don't disturb them," I said.

Taylor still didn't move, and I really wanted to DO this.

"Taylor," I said, "picture how scared Billy will be when HE goes up there. You KNOW how he is! This is even BETTER than our original plan!"

I guess that worked, because she let out a big sigh and followed me back in and back up the stairs and to the attic door. I whispered to her that we might want to crawl, and so we flattened ourselves onto the floor and scooted in and arranged the bones so they looked kind of like a human. No bats seemed to care about us, even though Taylor sneezed at one point. I saw it coming, so I put my hand over her mouth JUST in time. (Kind of yucky, yes, but that's the kind of thing best friends do for each other.) And even when I crawled to the far side of the room to open the window, they still just hung there upside down from the rafters and didn't move.

"Why did you open the window?" Taylor asked when we were back in the yard. We were brushing all the dust and stuff off of each other.

"So I can hear Billy scream," I said.

We both laughed.

Norka came over about then, and we went to the grocery store.

All Taylor and I wanted was a jar of jam.

That's all.

Nothing else.

How long do you think we were at the grocery store?

TWO HOURS! I SWEAR!!!!

Norka had never taken Grandma grocery shopping before, it turns out. And my guess is she'll never take her grocery shopping AGAIN! Once Grandma got in the store, she TOTALLY forgot that she lived with us, and she couldn't figure out WHY she needed any of the stuff Norka was getting.

It started like this. Norka put some stuff in the cart — I think it was a head of lettuce and a tomato. Then Norka turned to another shelf to grab a bunch of bananas. And when she turned back to put the bananas in the cart, the lettuce and tomato were gone. So Norka asked, "Where are the lettuce and tomato?" And Grandma, because she couldn't remember that she just put them back on the shelf, answered, "What lettuce and tomato?" And Norka said, "We need lettuce and tomato to make taco salad for the kids." And Grandma said, "What kids?"

AND IT WAS LIKE THAT THE WHOLE TIME!!! It was like shopping with Ren and Stimpy! Taylor and I TRIED to keep the stuff in the cart, but we kept getting into arguments with Grandma, and finally we just started letting her put the stuff back on the shelves, and then we would grab it back OFF the shelves and put it in the cart when she wasn't looking. It was TOTALLY confusing, and in the end there were a bunch of grocery store people following us around and helping us keep things in the cart (which was TOTALLY EMBARRASSING), and STILL there were a lot of things on the list that we didn't get. Of course, we didn't figure that out until we were home, in the kitchen, unpacking the bags.

AND DO YOU KNOW WHAT ONE OF THE THINGS WE FORGOT WAS? THE STRAWBERRY JAM!!!!

Norka offered to take us back (because she is very nice), and Grandma said she'd go and help (because she's very nice, too, even though she's SO frustrating sometimes!), but Taylor and I both yelled, "NO THANKS!" at the same time, and we grabbed a bottle of ketchup out of the refrigerator and said we'd have that instead of jam. Norka gave us a pretty weird look because she didn't know what we had planned to do with the jam in the FIRST place, of course.

It wasn't gloppy like the jam, but it would do.

I filled a cat dish with cat food, and we took that and the ketchup and we headed over to Mr. Owen's house again. Milky Way followed after the food, all the way up the stairs, although he was pretty slow on account of his belly being huge. Taylor crawled back into the attic and squirted ketchup onto the bones, but I stayed in the hall and just slid the cat dish inside the attic door. Milky Way didn't go to the bowl, though. He went right to the KETCHUP and started LICKING it off the bones! I started laughing, and Taylor turned all red from trying not to laugh, and she crawled back out, and we ran all the way down the stairs and out the back door again, laughing so hard we couldn't even talk.

It was SO perfect! The bats were a great touch we hadn't planned on, and Milky Way (Mr. Owen's "ghost") was licking "blood" off the bones!

We went around to the front of my house and sat on the grass where we had a view of the front of Mr. Owen's house AND the attic window. When we saw Billy's parents' car pull up (PERFECT timing — EVERYTHING was so PERFECT!) we made ourselves stop laughing by pinching each other, and Taylor got up, ready for her part.

"Hey, silly Billy," she called out in that same kind of singsong voice he uses with me, "I DARE you to go up in the attic!"

"So I can see Mr. Owen's son?" he said. He rolled his eyes and walked into the house behind his parents.

We waited.

It didn't take long.

We high-fived each other when we heard the scream, and both said, "YES!" at the same time when we saw a couple of bats actually fly OUT of the attic window. (We were so excited that we didn't say "Jinx" when we said that at the same time, which might be why the rest of the things happened.)

But when we heard a clunking sound, and AN-OTHER scream that turned into a lot more screams (which definitely sounded like there was some PAIN going on), we stopped celebrating and just stared at each other. We weren't sure what was happen-ing, but we knew it sounded SERIOUS and we knew we were probably in BIG TROUBLE.

Seconds later, Billy flew out the door.

"GET IT OFF ME!" he cried, swinging his arms all around, trying to get away from a bat that had flown out of the house right behind him.

His parents and the real estate agent raced out the door then, and his mom started screaming.

"He's bleeding!" she yelled, and that made Billy even more hysterical, and he wiped his face and held a red and drippy hand in front of him. Then he collapsed on the ground, screaming that he was going to die from rabies.

Other bats flew out the door just about then and Billy's mom swatted at one with her gigantic purse. Then she yanked that red-and-white "FOR SALE" sign out of the ground and chased the stunned bat across the lawn to a nearby tree, swinging the sign the whole way. The real estate agent — ducking so she wouldn't get hit — tried to pull the sign away from Billy's mom as she ran.

It was already looking a whole lot like an episode from *Malcolm in the Middle,* when my mom arrived home from work. She saw what was going on right away, I guess, because she stopped her minivan right in the middle of the street and ran up to the front of Mr. Owen's house. First she knelt down next to Billy, but she left him pretty quickly, and ran over to see what his mom was swinging at with the sign. And when she saw that it was a little bat, I could see her face get very red. My mom takes wildlife very seriously. When she spoke, she tried to keep her voice calm at first, but BOY, I could tell she was MAD.

"There's no need to do that," she was saying, trying, along with that real estate agent, to get hold of the sign. "Bats are beneficial creatures — they eat mosquitos — they don't harm people —"

Well, I don't think Billy's mom really wanted to hear the bat lecture. She held the sign up over my mom, like she was going to hit her!

"That thing BIT my son!" Billy's mom shrieked. "Look at him! He could have rabies."

Billy was sitting there, hunched over, still whimpering. Lots of people were looking at him, because by then my dad and Meghan and Emma and Grandma and Norka had all come out to see what was going on. Some neighbors started to appear in their yards, too.

And THEN Milky Way waddled out of Mr. Owen's front door, his white fur all splotched with red. And Taylor and I stood there, mouths wide open, as he went right up to Billy and started LICKING his face! I heard a scream behind me, and looked back to see Meghan running into our house.

"That's not BLOOD!" my mom yelled. "It's KETCHUP! The bat didn't bite your son. And it didn't give him rabies."

Billy's mom stopped being a maniac all of a sudden, and sort of froze there, so my mom grabbed the sign from her and threw it across the yard. (And the real estate agent ran after it.) And then the litte bat flew back into the attic through the open window. Suddenly everyone was really still and quiet. Even Billy.

"What happened up there Billy?" his dad asked him.

"I tripped over that cat," he cried, pushing Milky Way away from him. "It was DARK up there!"

"But WHY do you have KETCHUP on your face?" his mother asked him.

Billy turned his ketchup-covered face toward us, and pointed a ketchup-covered finger. "They did it," he said.

And everyone out there — which seemed like an awful lot of people — turned their heads and looked at us, too.

"Uh-oh," Taylor whispered.

"Adios," I whispered back.

The last two things we did together were (1) clean Mr. Owen's attic; and, (2) apologize to Billy.

bUt dOEsN't ReVeNgE RoCk aNyWaY?

We didn't mean to scare Billy THAT much. Really. We didn't want anyone to get hurt. I mean it. (Well, that's just tough if you don't believe me.)

Do you know what? Billy and his family haven't been back since last Monday. I'm hoping they decided not to move here, but I'm afraid to ask my mom or dad. It's better if I don't bring the whole thing up right now. Even though I'm pretty sure my mom isn't looking forward to getting to know Billy's mother anymore.

I need to take a break from all this writing! When I get back, I will begin working on cracking the code again. I think I might have what I need now!

|-)

July 25, Tuesday

I have some good news, some bad news, some more bad news, some more good news, and some more bad news. And I'm going to tell you about it all in this serious font. I'm feeling very serious. Soon you will know why.

Here is the first good news:

I have cracked the E-mail code. During my beached week, Dad helped Emma find the "missing" secret code book. He said it really was lost, it was under about a hundred Beanie Babies in the corner of her room. He said I should stop suspecting Emma of plotting against me. That she's my sister, and I should trust her. Hmm . . .

Well, the code book is GREAT, and (since I had so much extra time on my hands) I figured out how to do LOTS of cool note-folding, which I can't wait to do when school starts again. But about the codes . . . there were about ten of them in the book, and I studied them all and decided that only about three of them were possibilities for my E-mails, because the rest of them used numbers. My messages have no numbers, which is about all I could remember about them until I was able to print them out today.

The code in the book that was closest to my code is called a "Right Shift Alphabet Code," and this ALMOST worked. To make that code you shift one alphabet letter to the right. And to decode, you shift one letter to the LEFT (duh!). If you have to go to the left of the letter *A* then you go to *Z*, like the alphabet is one big loop. When I tried this code on the first E-mail, this is what happened:

Modz Hiitaz,
E dup'v xuev vi ca zios pax paehjcis!
Cemm

became

Lncy Ghhszy,
D cto'u wtdu uh bz yhnr ozw ozdgibhr!
Bdll

120

More nonsense, right? Well, there was one thing that stuck out. That first word *Lncy* looked awfully close to another word I know. Like my name. I thought that couldn't be a coincidence, and that I HAD to be close. So I went to Dad and I showed him what I had, and he said that maybe not all letters shift the same way, and that maybe even some go two spaces in one direction while others go three spaces in the other direction, or by some other pattern. So when I tell you that it took me HOURS to crack this code, you should understand that it's NOT because I'm dumb. It's because it was a hard code to figure out!!! I'm calling it the "Tug of War Code" because it goes in both directions at the same time. This is how it works. . . .

Consonants shift RIGHT one space, and vowels shift LEFT one space. You have to make two separate alphabet lines to do this code — one for consonants and one for vowels (and Y is on the consonant line, that's just the way it is). SO, to DECODE you have to shift LEFT one space for all the consonants, and RIGHT one space for all the vowels. "Modz" becomes "Lucy." And the word after it, "Hiitaz," becomes (oh, I HATE that nickname!!) "Goosey." And I guess you've figured out what THAT means . . .

The screen name "FUSVJ" translates to

"DARTH," which is Billy's screen name (or at least his OLD screen name). That's the first bad news. The messages are from Billy. (Grrr.)

I'll print out the two alphabet lines here, and decode all the messages, even the new one I got while I was beached last week. And that will reveal the second bad news and the second good news. You'll see . . .

Consonants:

B C D F G H J K L M N P Q R S T V W X Y Z

Decoded:

Z B C D F G H J K L M N P Q R S T V W X Y

Vowels: A E I O U

Decoded: E I O U A

Message #1:

> Modz Hiitaz,
>
> E dup'v xuev vi ca zios pax paehjcis!
>
> Cemm

Translation:

> Lucy Goosey,
>
> I can't wait to be your new neighbor!
>
> Bill

122

(For the rest of the translations, I'm not writing out his name — YUCK! And I'm NOT writing out that horrible "Lucy Goosey.")

Message #2:

E dup'v xuev opvem Nipfuz!

Translation:

I can't wait until Monday!

That, of course, was written BEFORE he came out for the Monday attic visit. And HE thought I was going to be the tormented one!

Message #3:

Zio lpix xji huwa na zios A-nuem uffsatt? Zios catv gseapf, Vuzmis!

Translation:

You know who gave me your E-mail address? Your best friend, Taylor!

That's the second bad news — betrayal by my

best friend. (My ex-best friend, that is.) It doesn't get a whole lot lower than that, does it? And, of course, it's not the first time. The first time was . . .

VaLeNtiNe'S DaY

At the beginning of the school year, Billy and I were sort of, kind of, actually going out. That means we talked on the phone sometimes and sat together sometimes during recess. We even went to the movies once, to see *Star Wars*.

It was like that right up until Valentine's Day, and I was hoping maybe he'd get me one of those little crystal power bracelets. I had my eye on a blue one, and he knew that.

Well, Valentine's Day came, and Billy arrived at school with a box, all wrapped up, and I knew he was going to put it on my desk. But — RIGHT IN FRONT OF EVERYONE — he walked right past my desk and straight to Taylor's, and he put the box on her desk.

And she just opened it (and didn't seem surprised, really), and it had (yes, you guessed it) a little crystal power bracelet in it.

Blue.

And she put it on and then SMILED at Billy.

I have never had to fight harder to keep tears

back, and I'm really very good at that. Only a few tears escaped, I think, but EVERYONE was looking at me. The WHOLE class. It was SO embarrassing.

Taylor always said she didn't know he was going to do that. But they were together for a few weeks (actually, two weeks, one day, and four hours) and Taylor and I didn't talk at all during that time, and then he did something equally mean to her and became Ashley's boyfriend.

Taylor was real upset, and I was real upset, and we decided that Billy wasn't worth our friendship being messed up, and we tried to forget about the whole thing, and to forget about Billy. Of course, we saw him every day in school, and he always tried to get our attention, but we had this pact, and we just pretended he wasn't there. Until he started thinking about moving to Oak Street, that is.

Things were desperate then. And we had to work together.

Or so I thought.

tHe EnD oF tHAt StORy
(AnD oF a FriEnDsHip)

Can you believe Taylor gave him my E-mail address? I'm SO bummed. :-{

I'm going to decode the last mystery E-mail now, which came last week while I was beached. It has the second good news in it . . .

Message #4:

> Xa'sa piv niweph vi lul Tvsaav. Xa giopf u cavvas jiota.
> Cz vja xuz, E xutp'v tdusaf.

Translation:

> We're not moving to Oak Street. We found a better house.
> By the way, I wasn't scared.

Yeah, right, he wasn't scared.

Good news about him not moving to Oak Street, huh? I wonder if Taylor knows. No, I don't. I forgot for a second that I don't care about her. She's at her mom's house this week, which makes it easier to be not speaking to her. I'm ignoring her E-mails and IMs and phone calls. I hear "Help!" and "Crazy" but I just listen to the songs. I don't change screens to check the messages. I just DON'T.

I've got a lot to do, anyway. Before my mom

left for work today, she gave me a list of things to pack. Which brings me to the last bad news. . . .

I'm leaving for camp on Sunday.

Ugh!

Why do I need to start packing today if I'm not leaving until Sunday?

That's dumb.

% (

July 29, Saturday

I'm going to the animal shelter in a little while. I'm hoping it will distract me from thinking about camp. I'm so nervous!!!!

I'm all packed. You wouldn't have BELIEVED the list. It had, like, five billion things on it. Three swimsuits, a water bottle with a strap, sunscreen, bug spray, two hats, two pairs of sneakers (argh!), flip-flops, two beach towels, two washcloths, ten pairs of underwear, and on and on and on and on and on and on and on and on and on and on and on and on and on and on. AND I had to put my name on EVERYTHING.

NOW I know why I had to start on Tuesday.

And you know, there wasn't only a list of things to PACK, there was a list of things NOT to pack. Like food. Like candy! And I've been saving those Hugs that my mom and dad bought me (after they stole my candy) just so I could have them at camp! Mom says bears will come if you have food in your bags.

BEARS!!!!

Boy, I'm SO nervous about going!!! It's like there's a ferret in my stomach doing flips every second!! I keep tossing Hugs into my mouth to try to calm the ferret (like, what ELSE am I going to do with them?), but it isn't working. And I'm starting to feel sick. I keep telling myself that it will be good to get away, that I won't have to face Taylor (who will be getting back to her dad's any minute). I'm SO mad at her!!!! I don't want to see her at all.

Do you know the name of the camp we're going to? HEMLOCK MOUNTAIN! Isn't hemlock the name of a POISON?

Emma keeps telling me I have nothing to worry about. She's been to Scout camp, and she says nothing could be worse than that, and she survived. She told me that at Scout camp, the drinking water was RED and tasted like blood, and that everyone was throwing up all week and some people got so sick they had to be picked up by their parents. And she said at Scout camp, they went on a hike and someone stepped on a copperhead snake, which is POISONOUS! And the snake didn't bite the kid, it bit the COUNSELOR, who had to go to the hospital. Emma never saw her again. And then, Emma said, a rabid squirrel came into their cabin and took a bite out of a girl's lollipop. It was one of those big, swirly lollipops, and this girl had it hidden in her bag, wrapped in plastic, and she only took it out at night, after she was in bed in the dark, so no one would see it.

I told Emma to shut up.

I'm NOT in a good mood.

Emma said she was just trying to make me feel better about camp.

Right.

I guess I shouldn't sneak any Hugs into my duffel bag.

Meghan has been helping me a lot. She wrote my name on masking tape (about eight thousand times) and then I just had to put pieces of the tape on the clothes and stuff. I told her how homesick I was going to be, and she told me that she wished she had gone to camp when she was my age. She didn't go away until she was fourteen, she said, when she went on a trip to Europe with a bunch of other kids she didn't really know too well. She said she was REAL homesick, and she was so far away that she knew there was no way to get home. But in the end, she made great friends, and was real glad she went, and wished she were going away this summer. To a place with no books, she said.

"I'll personally watch out for all your stuff while you're gone," she told me.

"Thanks," I said. And I hugged her. I was going to miss her.

"And can some of my friends sleep in your room?" she asked.

I told her that was okeday. I'm not sure if that was such a good idea. Oh, well.

Grandma woke up today and started talking about the animal shelter. I guess since she's there so many days a week, she can remember it. At breakfast she asked what time her friend would get here to take her to the shelter. (She thinks Norka is a friend — well, I guess Norka kind of is, because she seems to really like being with Grandma, not just like she works for us.) Mom told Grandma that it's Saturday, and that Norka doesn't come on Saturday. She told Grandma that they would go to the animal shelter next week. Grandma went, "Hmm, okay," and then she didn't say anything for a minute or so while she had some coffee, and then she asked what time her friend would get here to take her to the shelter.

It's like the words that went in her head just slipped right back out of her ear. (I wish they did. Then we could scoop them up off the table and slide them back in and put a piece of cotton in to make them stay.) That conversation went on for at least ten minutes — round and round and round. There I was, sitting there eating cereal with a big wooden mixing spoon because we don't have any regular spoons anymore, and the Cheerios were slopping onto my lap, and I'd just had enough of it all.

"Grandma! Norka isn't coming today!" I said, pretty meanly.

I didn't care if my mom got mad at me. I figured she'd never see me again once I went off on the camp bus, anyway, because I was sure to get eaten by bears or something, so what did it matter WHAT I said?

Mom glared at me.

"Who's Norka?" Grandma asked.

I rolled my eyes.

"What time is my friend coming to take me to the animal shelter?" Grandma asked Mom.

I was about to yell at Grandma again, but just

then Mom decided it was time to stop the conversational merry-go-round. She said:

"I will take you to the animal shelter, Gert. We'll go after I take my walk, okay?"

Grandma was real excited and she stood up and said she was going to look for her purse, which was right on the back of her chair. Before we could say anything, Milky Way jumped up in the chair and started eating the toast she'd left on her plate.

"Has Pharaoh had supper?" Grandma asked.

"I'm done here," I said, picking up my cup and bowl. I dropped them in the sink and started to head upstairs.

"Will you go with us, Lucy?" Mom asked.

"No," I answered.

"Oh, I guess you want to be around when Taylor gets back to her dad's," she said.

(I figured the way my mom is that she'd find out Taylor and I were not friends anymore in about the year 3000.)

I thought about that, though. Taylor WOULD be back anytime, and I really don't want to see her. Being away from the house began to sound like a good idea, so I decided to go. We're leaving soon. If I avoid Taylor this whole day, then I won't have to see her again until I get back from camp. IF I get back from camp. Maybe I'll forget who she is by then. Maybe I'll even have a NEW best friend by then.

Yeah, and maybe I'll win a million dollars and a ferret ranch and tickets to an N'Sync concert. Sure.

Mom's calling me.

Maybe there are ferrets at the animal shelter.

L8R

ⒿⒿⒿⒿⒿⒿⒿⒿⒿⒿⒿⒿⒿⒿⒿⒿ

It's about 11:00 P.M. now, and I can't sleep. So I'll tell you about my last afternoon and evening at home. I'll call this story . . .

We'LL sEE (yOu LatEr)

The animal shelter is a neat place. The lady who works there, Olivia, is real nice. She told us that Grandma is the best volunteer they've ever had there, and that the cats get so much love because of her. I really was surprised. I didn't think Grandma could do anything normal anymore.

When we got there, Mom asked Olivia if she could walk a dog, and they went behind a door, where a whole lot of barking was going on. I stayed in the cat room and watched Grandma open all the cages. The cats were all meowing at her, and they jumped down and rubbed up against her legs. Then she sat on this little sofa and the cats all tried to get in her lap at the same time, but only a few could fit at once, so there were always cats falling off and cats jumping on. Two of the littlest ones ended up on her shoulders. It was funny!

I petted the cats for a while, then started wondering about whether or not there were ferrets. I didn't see any, but there were a few doors, and I was hoping maybe one led into a room with a hundred ferrets, which could all surround me like the cats did to Grandma.

I saw Mom flash by, pulled by a very big dog, straight through the lobby of the shelter and out the front door. Then Olivia came into the cat room, and I asked her about ferrets.

"We do have one today," she said. "She was brought here yesterday. Her owner is moving to an apartment that doesn't allow pets."

"YES!" I said.

Olivia opened a blue door that said EXOTICS, and I went through it, and in front of me was a cage with the most BEAUTIFUL, PRECIOUS, ADORABLE, DARLING ferret sleeping in one of those ferret hammocks. It was brown and black and white and had a little mask across its eyes.

"Is it a baby?" I whispered.

"She's a few months old," Olivia said. "Her name is Tessa."

"Tessa," I repeated, sort of feeling like I was in a dream. "Can I hold her?" I asked.

Olivia opened the cage and told me to go for it. I reached in, so carefully, talking softly to her as I scooped her into my hands. Tessa opened her eyes slowly and yawned and stretched (UNBELIEV-ABLY CUTE!!). She wasn't scared when she saw me. She just looked curious.

There were toys on the floor, and I sat down next to them, with Tessa in my lap. I bounced a ball, and Tessa leaped up to get it and swatted it around the room and then back to me. She's OBVIOUSLY the SMARTEST ferret in the world!!!!

We played and played. Mom said it had been a whole hour when she came in the room and told me it was time to go. It didn't seem like an hour to me! It seemed like a few minutes! And I'd forgot-ten all about camp, and Taylor, and everything. Tessa was magic!

Grandma actually liked Tessa, too. She made Grandma laugh when she did flips. Olivia told my mom that we should adopt Tessa, and I loudly agreed with her! Mom told her that we had a houseful of animals and people.

"But Mom!" I said. "I don't have any pets. I can take care of her!"

"It's work caring for a ferret," Mom said. "They need a lot of attention."

Like I don't know they need a lot of attention!!!!

Mom said she'd bring me back to see Tessa another time.

"But Mom!" I said. "I'm going to camp! Tessa will be adopted by the time I get back!"

"Maybe not," Mom said. "We'll see."

Why do grown-ups always say, "We'll see"? They should just say "No," or "Go away and leave me alone." That's what they mean, anyway.

"Grandma," I pleaded, "will you play with Tessa when you come to the shelter?"

"Of course, dear," Grandma said.

I knew it would be impossible for Grandma to remember that, and I was feeling really sad about it all. I bit my lip and walked out the door of the shelter. Olivia followed me and we stood out front and she told me that when she was a little older than I am, her grandmother moved in with her, and she had Alzheimer's, too.

I couldn't believe that!

Olivia said she remembered it being real hard, but now when she thinks about it, she's proud of her family for wanting to be with her grandmother even though she wasn't acting like herself anymore.

I didn't know what to say. I watched as Mom helped Grandma into the car. Grandma waved and called out *good-bye* to Olivia and told her that she had a lovely daughter. After a second I realized she was talking about me. That made me feel bad, that she didn't recognize me at all.

But Olivia laughed.

"You have to have a sense of humor," she said to me. "And be yourself. You're a nice person."

"No, I'm not," I said. "I'm not always very nice to Grandma."

Olivia put her arm around my shoulders. "There are lots of bad things about Alzheimer's disease," she said. "But there is something good. You get a lot of chances."

I didn't know just what she meant, and I guess I gave her a funny look.

"Your grandma doesn't remember when you say something mean. You get to always have a do-over, so you can get it right," Olivia said.

I hadn't thought about it that way.

"I'll remind your grandma to play with Tessa,"

she said, and she walked me to the car and told me to have a good time at camp.

I tried to think about Tessa the whole way home, but my thoughts of her just jumped right out of my head and into my stomach, where she flipped and flopped. My mind totally filled up with worry about camp again. All I could think was, "I'M LEAVING TOMORROW! I'M LEAVING TOMORROW! I'M LEAVING TOMORROW!"

I thought I was going to wig out!

"Mom," I pleaded, "if I really hate it at camp, will you come and get me?"

"You're going to love it at camp, Lucy," Mom said.

"But IF I don't, or IF I'm sick, you'll come and get me, WON'T you?" I asked.

"We'll see," Mom said.

I rubbed my stomach and closed my eyes and tried to think about something else.

When we got home, Mom got out and went around the car to help Grandma. I watched them walk up the little steps of our porch, going very slowly. Even after they'd gone into the house, I stayed in the car. I don't know why. I just stayed there in the backseat and looked out the window.

Taylor showed up while I was sitting there, but she didn't see me at first. She went up the walk and knocked on the door. My mom answered and pointed to the car. I locked the door and looked out the other window, pretending I didn't know that Taylor was out there. She knocked on the car window and yelled that she was real sorry, and that she didn't mean to give Billy my E-mail address, and that she wouldn't ever again let him come between our friendship. I never looked out the window at her, though. I kept my eyes fixed on the other side of the street, blinking and wiping my eyes whenever the houses started to look all blurry. When I was sure she was gone, I got out of the car and went into the house.

Grandma was having tea with Dad at the dining room table, and when she saw me she smiled and told me to come in and see her. I didn't feel like it, but I went in anyway.

Grandma told me how glad she was to see me, and she wanted to know how old I was, and what grade I was in now, and what I was studying in school. She also wanted to know what was in the big tank in the corner of the room.

Dad was looking at me with that waiting look that's the same as tapping your foot, and so I told Grandma that I'm ten, and that there's no school in the summer, but when there is school I like writing best. I told her that the tank in the corner of the room has a big corn snake in it, and that it belongs to Mom.

She asked if the snake had had supper, and I told her that I didn't know, because Mom feeds it. She asked what it eats and I told her it eats mice, which is disgusting, I think.

"Lucy's nervous about going to camp, Mom," Dad said, giving me a little hug around my middle.

That's when I started crying. And I mean CRYING. Tears were just FLOODING out, like I was a big human sponge that Dad was squeezing. I couldn't see at all — my eyes were like faucets, pouring tears out everywhere. And I wasn't even embarrassed, which really surprised me. It felt good, actually, like all I needed in the whole world right then was to cry.

Grandma hugged me and told me it was all right. She said she cried the first time she went to camp, too, and that she used to go to camp for the whole summer when she was my age.

"THE WHOLE SUMMER?" I spluttered.

I couldn't IMAGINE!

She said her camp had a big lake where they canoed and fished and swam. Once, she said, a boy grabbed her leg when she was swimming, and he twisted her knee accidentally. She said that's why she has a bad knee.

I told her that wasn't such a good thing that happened to her at camp.

She laughed and said she loved camp anyway. She said that camp was an important part of her life, and she wished she were there.

I suggested that she go to camp instead of me, and that made her laugh. My dad laughed, too. I even laughed a little.

I dried my face on my sleeve and asked Grandma if she remembered Tessa, and, of course, she didn't. Dad suggested I show Grandma some pictures, and I reminded him that my book was gone. Then I remembered the website, and I ran upstairs and printed out a few ferret pictures and took them back down to Grandma. I showed her, and then Dad suggested I hang them up in her room, so we hung one from the mirror in her bathroom, and one on the side of her TV, and one on the snack table that she keeps next to her rocking chair.

After that, I helped Mom and Dad make macaroni and cheese, because they wanted us to have a dinner that Emma and I both like. (Emma isn't at all nervous about camp, though, so I don't know why she gets to have a special dinner.) We made "dirt and worms" for dessert (you know, crumbled cookies mixed with chocolate pudding and gummy worms), and Mom and Dad gave us books. I got *My Side of the Mountain* and Emma got *Treasure Island.*

aNd tHat's hOw mY LaSt dAy aT HoMe EnDEd.

It's really, really late now. I'm super tired. We're leaving so early tomorrow morning, on a bus that comes to the high school down the street. I won't have time to write in you tomorrow, so I'll say good-bye now.

Good-bye.

If I'm still alive in three weeks, I'll write in you then.

:'-(

Subj: **CaMp!!!**
Date: 08/04/01 04:12:51pm Eastern Daylight Time
From: Campers@HemlockMountain.org
To: FERRETLOVER@LEJ.COM

U'd think my mom would have at least MENTIONED that
this camp has a COMPUTER LAB! We get 2 come in once
a week N play computer games N surf the web N E-MAIL
people! I've E-mailed Aunt Katey N a bunch of my friends
from school (NOT Taylor!), N my mom N dad, N Meghan.
Oh, yeah, N myself!

This camp is coed! N there's a dance 2-night. Emma has
found lots of friends — boys N girls. She doesn't pay much
attention 2 me, but that's okeday. I've met lots of new
friends of my own. We're going 2 exchange E-mail ad-

dresses B-4 we go home, N stay in touch N even try 2 see each other. This one girl I really like — Natasha — lives in Baltimore, which is where my cousins live, so I'll get 2 see her sometimes, I hope. N — believe it or not! — this other girl, Carrie, lives in MY NEIGHBORHOOD!!! She goes 2 a private school, so that's why I haven't seen her around B-4, but now we'll DEFINITELY hang out.

I haven't been homesick ONCE! I'm too busy all day, N then at night we talk N talk until we fall asleep. Emma's in the same dorm I'm in, but on the other side. I've been rock climbing (scary but AWESOME) on this mountain which is right next 2 the camp. I've been on the zip-line TEN times!!! It is SO COOL. U get all strapped in-2 this harness by the counselors (who R all REALLY NICE N FUNNY — they're all college students) N then U hold on, N take a ride over the trees, N U end up on the other side of a stream, where there R other counselors 2 get U out of the thing. It's like FLYING!

We hike N learn about stuff in the woods around the camp, but we also go on trips. We R going 2 Kings Dominion next week!! I'm going 2 ride ALL the roller coasters this time!! Yesterday we were going 2 go 2 a swimming pool, but it rained in the afternoon, so we all went 2 the mess hall N baked cakes. Then we 8 them!!!

I want 2 LIVE here!!!

G2G. I want 2 play this cool computer game where U get 2 build YUR own amusement park.

Lucy

There's a science lab at this camp, too, N yesterday I was
in there. Last week in the lab we dissected owl pellets,
which R these cocoony-looking things that owls throw up
after they eat. How disgusting is THAT? U take the pellet
apart with tweezers N other pointy tools, 2 try 2 figure out
what the owl 8. Like with mine, I found all these bones inside the pellet, N I put all the pieces together like a puzzle,
N in the end it turned out 2 B a skeleton of a mouse. That
was the WEIRDEST N GROSSEST experience.

Kings Dominion was the COOLEST! Well, actually it was
the HOTTEST. It was 100 degrees ALL day, N sunny. Je-

remy, the counselor who was with our group, made us drink water every minute. They were giving free cups of water out at the park the whole day. I guess they didn't want people getting heatstroke while they were at the top of a roller coaster! I DID ride EVERY roller coaster!!! Carrie N Natasha went on all the rides with me. We did all the water rides about a hundred times, too.

There's this TOTALLY STRANGE boy — Jason — who's always following the three of us EVERYWHERE, N showing off. The other day he picked up this garter snake that was on the path when we were on a hike. The snake bit him, of course, N it would NOT let go. He was shaking his hand around N screaming, N the snake's body was flying all over the place, N finally one of the counselors squeezed the snake's head N that made it open its mouth wide enough so it let go of Jason. He had this bloody gash on his hand, though, which obviously hurt a lot from the way he was yelling. THEN, later the SAME day, someone dared him 2 pick up a yellow jacket, and he actually DID it!!! Of COURSE it stung him. Right on the end of his finger. What a BOZO!

I'm going 2 surf 4 a while. I need 2 see some pictures of ferrets, so I'll go 2 my FAVORITE website. I wonder how Tessa is doing.

Lucy

Subj: **A LITTLE HOMESICK**
Date: 08/18/01 04:38:09pm Eastern Daylight Time
From: Campers@HemlockMountain.org
To: FERRETLOVER@LEJ.COM

We've been stargazing this week, N 4 some reason, looking up at the stars makes me feel lonely. The universe is so
very, very huge, N we're so very tiny. Thinking about that
makes me feel homesick. N the counselors have been
telling scary stories around the campfires this week. I think
they figure, since it's the last week here, we won't B so
scared. Tory told this story about some crazy guy who always wears a pink bunny suit N goes into camps L8 at
night N tries 2 get into people's tents or dorms. Freaky. She
said it was true.

I've been thinking about Taylor a lot this week. I don't know Y. Well, I do, I guess. I miss her a lot. Even though she's not my friend N-E-more. She did apologize 2 me, though. Maybe I should have accepted her apology. It will be weird to start school without a best friend — especially since Taylor was the best best friend. Was.

Last night I couldn't sleep, N when all the people on my side of the dorm were asleep, I tiptoed across 2 the other side 2 see Emma. She was awake, even though all the other people on her side were asleep. She was reading *Treasure Island*, N I noticed that she was almost done with it. I thought that was strange, since I hadn't seen her reading, until now, N because I hadn't even gotten around 2 opening the book Dad gave me. I asked her if she couldn't sleep because of the pink bunny man, N she laughed N said there was no such thing as the pink bunny man. (That made me feel better.) I told her I was homesick, N she said she'd been homesick every night the whole time we'd been there. (Boy, was I surprised!) I asked if I could get in bed with her, 4 just a few minutes, N she said okay. I snuggled next 2 her, like we used 2 do when we were little. (B-4 friends came along.) She went on reading, N I asked if she would read it out loud 2 me, N she said she would. The characters were mean N scary pirates, but I felt safe there. I don't remember falling asleep, but I woke up the next morning 2 the bugle that Dara (one of the counselors) blows at 7:00 each day.

I guess, maybe, Emma isn't such a bad sister.

Next time I write, I'll be home!! Just a few days . . .

Lucy

August 20, Sunday

I am home now. And the story of this day is called . . .

gO aHeAd AnD mOvE!

The camp bus got back at about 5:00 P.M. today, and Mom and Dad were waiting for us. I was so glad to see them! I LOVED camp, but I missed them, too.

My dad had put a whistle in the tailpipe of the minivan to celebrate our return, and it made a screaming kind of sound as we drove home. People were looking at us, and it was kind of embarrassing, but it was fun, too!

When we got to Oak Street, the first thing I noticed was a SOLD sign in front of Mr. Owen's house. I asked Dad if he knew who was moving in, and he told me to ask Taylor, that she knew more than he did. I reminded him that I wasn't speaking to Taylor, but just as I was finishing what I was saying, I noticed that Taylor was sitting on the steps in front of our house. And do you know what she had in her arms? A KITTEN!

I figured I could talk to her this once.

"What's its name?" I asked, sitting next to her and petting the gray-and-white stripey kitty.

"Ron," Taylor answered.

"Ron? What kind of name is THAT for a cat?" I asked, laughing.

Taylor laughed, too. "First I named him Rontu, like the dog in *The Island of the Blue Dolphins,* but then I decided I liked Ron better."

"Oh, THAT makes a lot of sense," I said.

We laughed about that.

It was really nice to be laughing with Taylor, but it still felt weird. I was happy to see her, but I was still hurt that she'd given Billy my E-mail address.

"So, someone bought Mr. Owen's house," I said.

Taylor nodded.

"Did you meet them?" I asked.

"Sort of," she said. "I don't know if you'll like them."

We just sat there. It was kind of uncomfortable. I felt like saying something, but I didn't know what to say. I looked around the block. It was nice to be back on Oak Street. I looked from house to house, at the mailboxes and trees and front doors that make our street the way it is. And then I noticed it. The red and white FOR SALE sign. It was in front of Taylor's house!

"You're moving?" I asked, trying to sound calm, like I wasn't in any kind of panic or anything.

"Yeah, Dad finally decided it was time to move to a smaller house," she said, just like that, like she wasn't upset at all. Like she had TOTALLY gotten over our friendship being over!

I had a very big lump in my throat, and I wished I could go back in time to that day before I left for camp, and accept Taylor's apology. She would NEVER have let her dad move if we were still best friends. How could I have been so stupid? How could I have let that dumb thing with Billy wreck our friendship again? And this time it would be forever!

"Ron came from the shelter," Taylor was saying in a normal voice, like it was just any normal day and any normal conversation. "Your grandma helped me and my dad pick him out."

I decided to swallow the lump in my throat. I would be like her. I would NOT CARE. "Is the ferret still there?" I asked.

I had to have Tessa now, I figured. How else was I going to be able to get over losing my best friend?

Taylor shook her head. "She was adopted."

WHY did I come back from camp? I asked myself.

"Her name was Tessa," I said. "I wanted her SO bad."

"I know," Taylor said.

"How did you know?" I asked.

"Like, DUH!" Taylor said. "EVERYONE knew!"

She picked up Ron and started to walk in the house, so I followed her.

Grandma was in the living room on the couch with Milky Way asleep next to her. He looked even fatter than he did three weeks before. His eyes looked over at me, but he didn't move. I wondered if he'd finally gotten too fat to lift himself up.

"SHH!" Grandma whispered. "You'll wake Pharaoh!"

"Hi, Grandma," I said, giving her a kiss. "Do you know who adopted Tessa?"

"Who's Tessa?" Grandma whispered.

"You know, Grandma, the ferret at the animal shelter?"

"They don't have parrots at the shelter, dear," Grandma answered.

"Let's go up to your room," Taylor said.

I wasn't sure I wanted to go up in my room with Taylor. We obviously weren't really friends anymore. She obviously didn't care about me or my feelings. Not if she thought my losing Tessa was no big deal. And not if she thought that we could make up just like that, and then she could move away. She started up the stairs, though, so I followed behind her. Then we heard Meghan and some of her friends running down the stairs from the attic, so Taylor and I flattened ourselves against the wall and waited for them to pass us.

"Hey, Lu!" Meghan said. "Welcome home! Thanks for letting us use the room. And sorry about the broken mirror. I'll get you a new one, I promise. And, oh yeah, congratulations!"

"My mirror?" I asked, but she was out the door already. "Congratulations for what?" I called after her.

Taylor grabbed my arm and pulled me up the rest of the steps and into my room, and I looked over to where my full-length mirror had been, next to my desk. It wasn't there. I hoped I wasn't going to get the seven years of bad luck — I wasn't the one who broke the mirror.

Then I looked at my computer, which had a big sign taped to it. It read "I'M SORRY FOR BEING STUPID, PLEASE BE MY BEST FRIEND AGAIN. I'LL DO WHATEVER YOU SAY FOR THE REST OF YOUR LIFE. I WON'T LET ANYTHING COME BETWEEN US, TAYLOR."

"But you're mov —" I started to say, but then I noticed something ELSE there in my room.

A cage.

A tall, gray cage with a pointy roof.

And in the cage was — TESSA!!!!

"I CAN'T BELIEVE IT!!!" I cried.

Mom appeared at the door then with my duffel bag.

"Oh, thank you, thank you, thank you!" I yelled, and hugged her.

"Grandma adopted her for you," she said. "With a lot of help from Taylor." She gave Taylor a look that was sort of stern, but sort of joking.

Taylor started babbling about how her dad took her to the shelter to get a kitten because she was so sad about messing up our friendship, and when she was there she saw Grandma, who was playing with Tessa, and she figured that if I got a ferret I'd be SO happy that I'd forget to be mad at her anymore, and I'd be her best friend again, and so she begged and begged Grandma to adopt her for me, and Grandma actually DID.

Taylor's words were flitting around the room like butterflies. I sort of heard them, I sort of didn't. I was in a trance. I opened the gray cage and reached in and took sleepy Tessa out. She stretched and yawned. I held her against me.

"I was going to take her back to the shelter right away," Mom said. "But, you know, she's kind of a cute little thing."

Dad and Emma came into my room then.

"This is SO not fair," Emma said. "I want a new pet."

"But you already have a turtle and a toad," Mom said.

"Do you think Grandma could adopt a puppy for me?" Emma asked.

"Hmm, we'll see," Mom said.

I felt sorry for Emma.

"You can come in and play with her whenever you want," I told her.

"Why don't you go show Grandma that weasel?" Dad said to me.

I ran downstairs and found Grandma in the

kitchen slicing a donut into Milky Way's dish. She leaned down and put the cat dish on the floor and then walked over to the trash can and dropped the knife in.

I opened the silverware drawer, expecting to find nothing in there, and instead it was filled to the top with silverware — all old, like it came from yard sales. Mostly spoons.

Just then, Tessa leaped from my arms right onto Grandma's shoulder.

She laughed real loud.

Then I laughed.

"Grandma, thanks so much!" I said, pulling Tessa off her shoulder.

"Thanks for what?" Grandma asked.

"For THIS!" I said, holding Tessa out for Grandma to pet her.

"What is it?" she asked.

"TOTAL HAPPINESS!" I answered.

"That's a funny name," Grandma said, and she ran some water in the sink and started scrubbing some dirty dishes.

There weren't any suds at all, and I thought I should go get Mom so she could help Grandma, but then Tessa leaped out of my arms again, right onto the kitchen counter. She bumped into the container of pink dish soap, which slid over into the sink.

"Oh, isn't that fun!" Grandma said, scooping up the suds that were bubbling up in the sink.

"Good job, Tessa," I whispered in Tessa's ear as I lifted her off the counter.

(See? Isn't she the smartest ferret in the world?)

"So how old are you now, dear?" Grandma asked me. She had a lot of suds going now and was squirting more soap into the water. I knew it was too much, but I didn't say anything.

"I'm ten, Grandma," I said. "And you know what else I am?"

"What else?" she answered.

"I'm glad you're here. REALLY!" And I hugged her with my free arm.

I knew she wouldn't remember I said that, but I planned on saying it again some other time, many other times.

Taylor called me from the front door and said she had something to show me, so I followed her outside. I held Tessa and Taylor held Ron, and they were very curious about each other, sniffing and nipping and wanting to play. But we held onto them because we didn't want them to run off and get hurt.

"Thanks SO much for helping me to get Tessa," I said. "And I'm sorry about what happened. I was being stupid."

"No, I was being stupid," she said.

"No, I was being stupid," I said.

We laughed.

We like to laugh.

"So we're best friends again?" Taylor asked.

"And we'll never let anything come between us again?" I asked.

"Never," Taylor said. "And especially not Billy."

"So PLEASE tell your dad you don't want to move!" I cried.

"My dad already found a house he really likes," she said. "It's smaller, and it's real nice. I kind of like it, too."

"But will I ever see you? Will you go to the same school? Can I walk to your house?" I asked, crossing my fingers that the anwers would be yes to all of the above.

Taylor nodded. "Yes, yes and yes. I'm going to show you my new house right now. Follow me."

And she walked down the front steps, and turned onto the sidewalk, and walked about twenty steps and then stopped in front of Mr. Owen's house.

"We're moving THERE," she said, pointing right at Mr. Owen's door.

"No WAY!" I yelled.

161

"Yes WAY!" she yelled back.

"I CAN'T BELIEVE IT! This is TOO COOL!" I yelled.

And we high-fived each other, and I guess I wasn't holding onto Tessa very well, because she leaped onto the ground, and I guess Taylor wasn't holding Ron so well, because HE leaped down onto the ground, and the two of them started chasing each other down the street.

We ran after them until we got to Taylor's yard, where Tessa had climbed up on the FOR SALE sign, and I took her back in my arms, and Taylor picked Ron back up, too. Taylor's dad came out of the house then.

"We have to leave for a little while," he said. "Someone's coming to look at the house right now."

And while we were still standing there a car pulled up, and that same real estate agent got out and opened a car door for this lady who also got out. She had a little girl in her arms.

"What a quiet, peaceful neighborhood!" she said, looking up and down the street.

Taylor and I looked at each other and laughed. We could tell that we were each thinking about that last day Billy was at Mr. Owen's house, and how NOT quiet and peaceful it had been on Oak Street.

"Do you girls live here on the block?" she asked us.

We nodded.

"How old are you?" she asked.

"Ten," we said, at the same time. (This time we said, "JINX!")

"Isn't that nice!" she said, and then the back door of the car opened, and a soccer ball came flying out into the yard, followed by a dark-haired, racing blur.

"He's ten, too!" the mother said.

"I think you'll like this house!" I heard Taylor say, and her eyes were on the boy dribbling the ball down the driveway and into the backyard. She was watching him a little too closely, I thought.

I stepped in front of her and gave her a look that said, "Let's not GO THERE."

She snapped out of it, and said to the boy's mother, "Or, maybe the house is too big."

And then ANOTHER dark-haired, racing blur flew out of the back of the car, chasing after the first one.

"They're twins," the mother said.

Taylor and I looked at each other with wide eyes. Then we just started laughing. We like to laugh.

Hey, I've got to go! I may not have a lot of time for writing for a while. I've got a ferret now, and, YOU KNOW, they need LOTS OF ATTEN-TION!

ThE eND

:'-D